Temmi and the Flying Bears

'We have been sent by command of the great Witch herself. She has heard of a rare thing found only in these parts. A bear with wings. And it is her noble majesty's wish to give one of these freakish creatures to her daughter, Princess Agna, as a pet.'

Temmi is horrified when the Witch Queen's soldiers march into his village and take one of the flying bears. And when he discovers that it's Cush who has been taken, Temmi's favourite bear cub, he sets out to rescue him.

But once Temmi reaches the frozen palace he realizes that his quest is more difficult than he'd first thought—in order to save Cush he must win over the ice-hearted Princess Agna . . .

Stephen Elboz lives in Northamptonshire, and has had a variety of jobs, including being a dustman, a civil servant, and a volunteer on an archaeological dig. He now divides his time between teaching and writing. His first book, *The House of Rats*, won the Smarties Young Judges Prize and his series of books about the young magician Kit Stixby have earned him great critical acclaim.

Temmi and the Flying Bears

Other books by Stephen Elboz

Temmi and the Flying Bears

Stephen Elboz

Illustrated by Lesley Harker

OXFORD
UNIVERSITY PRESS

OXFORD
UNIVERSITY PRESS

Great Clarendon Street, Oxford OX2 6DP

Oxford University Press is a department of the University of Oxford.
It furthers the University's objective of excellence in research, scholarship,
and education by publishing worldwide in

Oxford New York
Auckland Bangkok Buenos Aires
Cape Town Chennai Dar es Salaam Delhi Hong Kong Istanbul
Karachi Kolkata Kuala Lumpur Madrid Melbourne Mexico City Mumbai
Nairobi São Paulo Shanghai Taipei Tokyo Toronto

Oxford is a registered trade mark of Oxford University Press
in the UK and in certain other countries

British Library Cataloguing in Publication Data available

ISBN 0 19 275259 6

3 5 7 9 10 8 6 4 2

Typeset by AFS Image Setters Ltd, Glasgow

Printed in Great Britain by
Cox & Wyman Ltd, Reading, Berkshire

In fondest memory of Gordon Blake

Chapter One

Now Temmi had a fondness for all the forest bears. He knew them as well as any hunter.

Cinnamon bears, he would tell you (or, better still, take you to his special place where you could see for yourself), were as nimble as monkeys, and climbed so quickly that they were soon lost from sight at the tops of the tallest trees; and their whines and whistles sounded so sad that he shivered whenever he heard them.

Sag bears couldn't be more different. Temmi often laughed aloud just to see one of these stupid creatures. They looked like fat, over-cooked puddings . . . and behaved rather like them as well! Too lazy to run away, they snoozed with their snouts on their chests, scratching themselves in their sleep and sending up a cloud of thick dust similar to when an old mat is beaten.

Then there were the growlers—huge, secretive bears that prowled the thickest parts of the forest. Temmi had learned to admire these dangerous creatures from a distance (or from up a tree), because growlers were so fierce that even a wolf pack would turn around rather than risk crossing paths with one.

But of all the bears, Temmi's best-loved by far were the flying bears.

Every day, after he finished helping his father bring in the fish from the lake, when the canoes were safely pulled up on the shore and the nets mended and hung up to dry, Temmi slipped away from his village and hurried into the mountains. Steadily he climbed until he reached the place where snow lay all year round, and icicles on rocky ledges might melt an inch or two in summer, but never completely disappear—just like his old footprints.

Then, on reaching a certain hill, he stopped to view the distant cliffs hoping to see a flying bear. Rarely was he disappointed. They were gloriously white bears both in fur and feathers—although the old ones might be nearer to ivory, the cubs were as bright as snowflakes.

Temmi was proud that he could recognize every flying bear in the colony, each bear having its own special ways; and it was Temmi who had given them their names. If you asked him he would tell you that Dorf barked like a seal; Snibpuss was nosy and always getting into trouble for it; Abany was vain, spending much of his time grooming himself; and Ocki was greedy and rather fond of stealing other bears' fish . . .

But Temmi's favourite was Cush, the last cub born that year, born so long after the other cubs that Temmi worried he might be too small to survive. His mother, Pasha, sat on her nest of twigs keeping him warm and feeding him her milk, yet she must have worried about her young cub too. She knew that Cush must be able to fly before the first snows came. And one day, as Temmi watched, he saw her gently nudge her cub to the edge of her nest high up on the cliff-side. Cush yelped and cried and tried to scramble back to safety, but Pasha was firm. With one final shove she sent her cub tumbling through the air.

Temmi gave a horrified gasp, but he need not have worried. Instinctively the little bear spread his downy wings and Temmi watched him gently glide to the nearest tree. There he landed, wildly scrabbling with his paws, and shaking down much snow. Once safe upon a branch, however, he looked so pleased with himself that Temmi broke out into applause.

The little bear gazed down at him, mouth open and tongue hanging out—amused in a kind of bear-like way. And Temmi beamed back, as proud of him as Pasha was.

After that there was no stopping Cush. He turned into a proper little show-off, especially if Temmi was around. Then he'd swoop and hover and loop-the-loop; and when Temmi saw his fur was wet he knew he'd been learning how to catch fish in the nearby river.

Soon Temmi was bringing him presents of fish he had stolen from his father's boat, being careful to hide them beneath his cloak. And Cush came to expect a fish every time he visited, although at first he was rather puzzled, wondering why the boy was holding up a fish in the air. Fish came from rivers, not boys, and they live in water, not air . . . But as Cush grew more used to Temmi and his confidence in flying grew, he would come diving down and gently take the fish in his paws, carrying it back to the cliff where he ate every bit, apart from the bones, fins, and tail (which Ocki came sniffing around for later on).

And this was how the friendship between Temmi and Cush first began.

Chapter Two

The men arrived at Temmi's village one snowy winter's evening. They stood in silence, watching with grim, hard faces. They carried spears, and alongside them were wolves—hunting wolves—to which the men spoke harshly, kicking them with their boots whenever fights broke out.

As head of the village, Temmi's father went out to greet them; Temmi went with him, a few paces behind, treading on his father's shadow and feeling a little nervous. The rest of the village looked on, unsure what to make of the men and wondering why they had come. The village dogs, however, had made up their minds already. They barked madly at the scent of so many wolves and had to be shut away. But Temmi, along with everyone else, knew the strangers must be made welcome. That was the rule of the village.

The leader of the strangers wore a heavy wolf-fur cloak over finer clothes. And yet Temmi hardly noticed anything of what he wore so astonished was he by the man's face. Or rather *his nose*, for it was made of silver and not like a human nose at all but more like a snout, complete with two tiny tusks carved out of walrus ivory. A black silk ribbon kept the false nose in place, tied in an elegant bow at the back of his head.

Finally the man spoke, his voice ringing out and sounding oddly hollow.

'My name is Lord Thurbolt,' he said with a brisk nod and click of his boot heels. 'I serve Haggoth, Witch-Queen of the High Witchlands. But should you wish it, the other name by which I am known is General Tin Nose.' He smiled slyly. 'They call me this even though none of my many noses is made out of tin.'

'*Many noses?*' said Temmi's father, confused.

In answer, Tin Nose called across one of his men. The fellow bowed and held out a small wooden box. Throwing his cloak over one shoulder, Tin Nose flicked open the lid.

Inside, Temmi was amazed to see a number of

different metal noses set into the velvet lining. Some were animal-like, some human—and some, he thought, wouldn't look out of place on the faces of trolls. But, as Tin Nose had boasted, none was of tin. They shone either gold or silver and many had the extra glint of a precious stone or pearl.

Tin Nose caught Temmi staring at him and lifted a hand to his face, saying, 'Perhaps you would care to see the hole underneath where my real nose used to be?'

Too horrified for words Temmi urgently shook his head.

Tin Nose let out a great roar of laughter and, lunging at the wolves that milled about his feet, seized the largest by the throat. The wolf bristled angrily and tried to turn his head to bite, but Tin Nose held him firmly and the best the wolf could do was make threatening growls.

'This is the villain,' he said. 'This is the devil who bit off my nose and swallowed it when he was still no bigger than a cub. Ah, Frostbite, I knew then what a fine hunting animal you'd be and I was right, although I had you severely beaten for what you did to me.'

He shook Frostbite as if strangling him, but in his rough play was affection as well as respect.

Temmi's father cleared his throat. 'You and

your men must be weary, Lord Thurbolt,' he said and he led the way to the longhouse where the villagers held their meetings and feasts.

Once inside, Tin Nose gazed around at the wooden benches and ancient shields upon the log walls; his feet kicked at the rushes upon the mud floor. Without saying a word he gave Temmi the impression he was used to better things. Then he stared hatefully at the blazing fire at the centre of the hall, turning sharply on his heels and striding away from it. Behind the long tables his men whipped the wolf pack into silence.

The meal that followed was an unhappy one. Tin Nose's men stared at the plates of baked fish and stewed cabbage, refusing to touch them. Some were heard to grumble, 'Have they no meat?'

Temmi and the other villagers ate in silence, glancing nervously at the wolves who were as scornful of the food set before them as their masters had been, pawing the fish, or throwing it up in the air like a child with a toy.

Giving a loud snort, Tin Nose finally shoved his plate aside; and Temmi heard one of the villagers whisper, 'They don't care for our food, they don't care for our company . . . so why are they here?'

Moments later they found out. Rising to his feet, Tin Nose spoke to them.

'I will speak briefly and plainly,' he said, as if the villagers were too stupid to understand anything else. 'I have been sent by command of the great Witch herself. She has heard of a rare thing found only in these parts. A bear with wings. And it is her noble majesty's wish to give one of these freakish creatures to her daughter, Princess Agna, as a pet.'

Hearing this, Temmi angrily jumped up. 'The flying bears aren't freaks!' he shouted. 'They are wild creatures—and you can't make a wild creature live in a cage. It will die of unhappiness!'

Tin Nose stared at him coldly, his metal nose winking in the centre of his shadowy face. 'The great Witch herself has ordered it,' he growled. 'And no one shall question her orders.'

'He is very young, my lord,' apologized Temmi's father, quickly pushing Temmi back down on the bench. And he hissed, 'Hush now, boy. Do you want to make the Witch so angry that she sends the snow and frosts against us? Do you want the lake to stay frozen all summer? Is that what you want? Nothing in your belly because we can't fish.'

'But I—'

10

'*Not another word*, do you hear?'

Temmi nodded sulkily, but his outburst had made matters between the strangers and villagers even more awkward than before. Secretly most of Temmi's neighbours agreed with him but they kept silent, afraid of the Witch-Queen's magic.

After the plates were cleared away, the villagers did their best to entertain their guests. But their efforts were wasted. Tin Nose openly yawned at the singing, shouting over it for his tankard to be refilled—treating the villagers as little more than servants. His men talked and laughed together as Croel played his harp.

Everyone was glad when it grew late and they had to return to their huts, leaving the strangers to bunk down in the longhouse, using the tables as beds.

Temmi went home with his father, too furious to speak, and threw himself down on his bed of straw. The flying bears weren't freaks—*they weren't* . . . On the bed next to his, his father snored, but Temmi turned restlessly.

Outside, the bitter east wind blew across the lake. Temmi listened to it rattle loose reeds in the thatch, he listened as it shook the door, then his eyelids grew heavy . . . and slowly he drifted off to sleep.

Chapter Three

Temmi awoke suddenly, a wolf's howl still ringing clear and terrible in the air.

It *hadn't* come from the longhouse.

Moments later a second wolf answered from the other side of the village.

A man shouted.

A woman screamed.

Snatching up his fishing knife, Temmi's father dashed out into the freezing night. Temmi followed, wrapped in his blanket, his breath frost-white in the moonlight.

'What is it?' yelled Temmi's father. 'What's happening?'

Cuddie the old fisherman came hobbling out of

the shadows. Temmi's father raised his knife higher until he recognized him and lowered it again.

'It's the Witch's men,' gasped Cuddie. 'They've upped and gone.'

'Gone?'

Cuddie nodded. 'The men have gone but not the wolves. The wolves are all around the village, driving our people back.'

Temmi's father scowled angrily. 'What on earth do they mean by this?'

But Temmi knew at once. 'They've gone after the flying bears!' he cried, and before either man could stop him he ran off into the darkness.

'Come back, boy!' he heard his father shout.

But Temmi ran on, past the huts and his dismayed neighbours who stood around in helpless groups, until he reached the ditch at the edge of the village. He saw it was as Cuddie had described. The wolves swept by in a straggling pack, some along the bottom of the ditch like shadows, those at the top with the gloss of the moon on their coats.

Suddenly—before he had time to do anything—a large dark shape broke away from the others and leapt at him. Temmi saw claws and fangs and a narrowed pair of yellow eyes—then the wolf's front paws struck his chest. He fell back shocked and winded. Then could not rise—the wolf was on top of him, and Temmi looked up into the jaws of Frostbite.

Slowly, taking pleasure from it, the great wolf sniffed him as if sniffing his next meal, his wet snout snuffling over Temmi's face. Sick with terror, Temmi remembered Tin Nose and how he had earned his nickname; and as if in a dream he pictured himself with his own metal nose. His father was too poor to afford silver. Perhaps he could make him an iron nose from an old cooking pot instead.

His paws still pressing heavily upon Temmi's body, Frostbite threw back his head and gave such a long eerie howl that it was as if he was trying to shatter the moon like glass; then he leapt off Temmi, turning in mid air, and raced down the bank and up the other side, until he was once more leading his snarling pack around the village.

Temmi sat up, too shaken to feel hurt. Next moment his father was there dragging him away.

'Stupid, stupid boy,' he blazed. 'What did you hope to do against the Witch's servants? Did you think they would be kinder to you because you are a child?' He ran his hand through his hair, growing more calm. 'Did they hurt you?' he asked at last.

Temmi shook his head. He knew his father had every right to be angry with him, especially as the wolves were running hungry. But he was not a baby, he could take care of himself. And he resented the way his father gripped his arm as they hurried to the safety of the longhouse where the rest of the villagers now were.

Inside, the air buzzed with excitement and confusion. Everyone was speaking at once, nobody listening to anyone else. Temmi noticed the men armed with fishing knives; and from the walls he saw the ancient shields being carefully handed down, the men ashamed by the dust on them.

Climbing on to one of the long tables, Temmi's father shouted and stamped his foot until everyone was silent. The villagers stared at him.

'I know you are angry,' he told them. 'You have reason to be. The Witch's men have treated us like the dirt on their boots—and now her wolves run wild, making us prisoners in our very own village. But going after them in the dark will only make matters worse. Wolves see better at night. They will split us up and hunt us down. For the sake of our safety I say we must stay together here in the longhouse. In the morning, if they have not gone, we shall drive them away with our knives.'

Heads nodded in agreement. The fire was built higher and the children were settled beneath the tables. By the door, men stood on guard. They gazed down at their knives and wished for swords.

Outside, the wolves bayed, one answering another from every point around the village—and sometimes from inside it too.

Temmi fell asleep sitting up against the longhouse wall. He awoke shivering as the men were getting ready to go out. He overheard them talking.

'The wolves have gone!' reported one man. 'I saw them race away into the forest just after dawn.'

The other men nodded and muttered together and said it was good news.

'Yes, but we must follow them,' said Temmi's father. 'We must be sure they have left our lands for good. They may be hiding in the forest. Nothing would make me happier than to find their tracks heading straight for the mountains.'

Hearing this, Temmi leapt up and tugged at his father's sleeve. 'Pa, Pa. Let me come with you. *Pl-ease*, Pa!'

His father looked sternly at him, on the point of saying no, but Donmar the carpenter said, 'Oh,

16

let the boy come. After all, he is nearly old enough to take out his own canoe on the lake.' And after a moment's thought, his father shrugged and let him.

'But don't whine or complain if you get tired or cold,' he warned. 'Now go and fetch my second-best knife for yourself, the one with the notched blade that I keep under my bed.'

Temmi grinned. 'Yes, Pa.'

He ran to his hut. The village was oddly silent. The cocks had not crowed for dawn because they were still shut away in the dark. Snatching up the knife from its hiding-place, Temmi raced back to join the men who had already started off from the longhouse.

They gathered at the ditch, gazing in silence at the endless rings of pawprints in the snow, and to prove to themselves that the wolves had really gone, they walked all around the village. At one point they saw the tracks break off and stream away into the forest.

'They're heading east,' said the blacksmith.

'*The flying bears!*' uttered Temmi.

'The bears can look after themselves,' said his father. 'Even if Tin Nose finds them he'll never be able to catch one. The flying bears are too clever for that.'

Despite his father's words, Temmi felt on the edge of something quite terrible. Tin Nose would never come all this way then simply give up . . . he would never dare return to the Witch empty handed . . .

They followed the tracks through the forest and up the steep slopes, walking in each other's footprints where the snow was deep.

'Look!' cried Cuddie pointing up.

A single flying bear flew high in the cloudless sky.

'Beog—' Temmi recognized the bear as Cush's father; and he noticed how Beog's head drooped and how every now and again he lifted it to give a long sad cry. This made Temmi even more uneasy; he kept running ahead and urging the men to hurry, getting angry with them when they didn't.

At last they arrived at the foot of the bears' nesting cliff—and Temmi knew for sure something was badly wrong. The bears sat silently on the ledges, wings folded, staring steadily down. Temmi had never known the bears as cold and unfriendly as this before, and then he saw the reason why . . . The splash of red blood and the hateful black arrow tipped with crow-feathers.

He yelled and bounded forward. If it wasn't for the blood, the dead bear might have been mistaken for another mound of snow, its wings half opened and crumpled beneath it.

It was Pasha.

Temmi gripped the black arrow that had taken her life. He gripped and pulled. The arrow had gone deep, but as his fury turned to strength, it came free. He broke it over his knee and casting the pieces away threw himself over Pasha's body, sobbing uncontrollably.

The men gathered round, watching him and feeling awkward.

Suddenly Temmi remembered Cush and clawing the tears from his eyes searched the ledges, desperate to catch sight of him.

'Cush! Cush!' he called at the top of his voice. But Cush was not there and Temmi suddenly understood; he understood that Pasha had been killed to lure her small cub to the ground. The simple truth was, the bears' cleverness had proved useless against cold cruelty, and Tin Nose had taken his prize after all.

The bears glared down at the boy who shouted up at them. All at once and together they broke into an angry barking, leaning over the ledges, some beating their wings. Their thoughts quite clear. Humans were murderers and takers of the young. Humans were *never* to be trusted.

Chapter Four

Temmi knew nobody understood how much the flying bears meant to him, not even his father. They thought the bears the same as any other wild creature—no different to the deer, the foxes, and the rabbits. They did not see how special they were. Now, as his father stepped forward and gently stroked his shoulders, Temmi shrugged off his hand, refusing to listen to anything he said.

Still, his father tried. He offered to let Temmi carry his best knife back to the village. He promised him bread spread thickly with honey (from their one pot of honey that had to last the whole winter). He promised to build Temmi his own canoe and give him five of his best fish-hooks.

But Temmi continued to sob and run his fingers through Pasha's fur.

After kindness failed, his father tried being firmer with him. 'Come on, Temmi, end all this nonsense,' he said bluntly. 'It's only a flying bear. One won't be missed. And at least the Witch's men have left our village in peace. Be thankful, boy, that they have gone.'

Temmi glared up with savage red-rimmed eyes. Without the Witch's men there, all his anger turned against his father for the thoughtlessness of his words. He leapt up and began to run, scrambling wildly through the snow.

'Come back, Temmi!' shouted some of the men.

'Oh, let him go,' sighed his father wearily. 'He is best left on his own for a while.'

The men turned and made their way back down to the village. But Temmi's father was wrong about his son. He had not run away to be alone, he had gone to follow the Witch's men and rescue Cush. It wasn't grief that drove him on, it was fury.

Even with his eyes blurred with tears, the tracks Temmi followed showed clearly in the snow.

Men's boot-marks and wolves' pawprints. The first stretching away in straight marching lines, the second scuttering busily between interesting smells: but both headed deep into the mountains. Temmi kept his eyes fixed on the tracks. He thought of Cush and sometimes of his father, but never once did he think of turning back.

Night came before he knew. The snow turned silver, then grey, and the tracks filled with darkness, like tiny pools of water. Only then did Temmi realize he was hungry and growing steadily colder. He lifted his head. In the distance he saw firelight. Tin Nose must have stopped to set up camp, the fire not for warmth or cooking, but to keep away the snow leopards and other wild creatures.

The light lay further off than Temmi had guessed, but as he finally crept up to it, dodging from one pine tree to the next, he heard Tin Nose talking to his men. 'Go get yourselves bedded down,' he barked. 'We set off before first light. You will need a good sleep for the long trek that lies ahead of us.'

The men shuffled away to dig themselves burrows in the snow, roughly calling the wolves to come to them and dragging the creatures into place before them like living doors. The wolves had been trained to obey, and laying their heads on their paws, went swiftly to sleep.

Temmi watched this safely from a distance. He knew from hunting in the forest that the first rule was to keep downwind of the camp, so the wolves didn't smell him there. Apart from the men and wolves, Temmi had also noticed a rough, hastily made cage. Inside it a small creature restlessly turned, now and again standing absolutely still to whimper and listen for its mother.

'Oh, poor Cush,' murmured Temmi, his heart going out to the little bear. 'He hasn't enough room to stretch his wings.'

He saw two moist brown eyes peer out through the bars; and certain that the rest of the camp was now asleep, Temmi crept up as silently as he could, which was not easy, for snow does not muffle footsteps, it creaks and groans, and the hard crust of frost upon it split and cracked like ice. At every step he waited for one of the wolves to raise its head. But the pack slept on and the men's snores sounded faint beneath the banks of snow.

At first Temmi's shadow was made by the blue light of a billion blazing stars, but as he neared the centre of the camp, the firelight stretched it longer and made it lean a different way. Temmi blinked through the flames. The wolves might

have been rugs spread over the snow so still did they lie.

By this time he was very close to the cage. He saw a snuffling nose poke from it, only to quickly disappear and reappear in another place—and another, until Cush was perfectly sure who he could scent. Then his entire rump waggled because his tail was too short and stubby to express all of his joy.

Temmi stretched out his hand and Cush frantically licked it in return. Smiling to himself, Temmi knew he must not forget the real reason he was there, and he hadn't much time. Seeing the cage door tied with string, he used his father's old knife to cut through it; immediately the door fell open and Cush came tumbling out.

He gazed up at Temmi adoringly, his back half still wagging.

'Go, Cush,' hissed Temmi. 'Fly away. Go home. Go back to Beog and the other bears.'

Cush bounded playfully around his feet. Across on the other side of the fire a wolf stirred.

Temmi was in trouble—he knew for sure he was going to get caught. But there was no reason why Cush should be caught with him. Not caring now about the noise he made, he snatched up the little bear and flung him high into the air.

Cush hovered looking puzzled. Was this a game? Deciding that it was, he came gliding back down to earth.

That same moment a ferocious-looking wolf sprang through the flames of the fire, its pointed teeth snapping shut like a trap around Cush, even before Cush could touch the ground.

'*No!*'

A shout ripped out of Temmi—then men and wolves came running.

Chapter Five

Tin Nose led the dash, looking startlingly different in a silver nose as pointed as any dagger. He swept down upon Frostbite giving such a bellow that everyone else stood still. Then with the flat of his sword still in its scabbard, he struck the wolf a heavy blow across his back. Frostbite's mouth sprang open to yelp, and a white ball of fur and feathers dropped to the ground.

Temmi scooped Cush up, holding him tenderly in his arms. Cush, wet with wolf-spit, trembled and whimpered, and one of his wings trailed like a broken fan, unable to close. Temmi touched it and Cush squealed with pain.

Tin Nose hovered over them like a storm about

to break, his drawn sword flashing in his hand. 'I ought to kill you here and now for the trouble you've caused,' he said fighting back his rage.

Although trembling and afraid, Temmi met his glare full on. 'This is your fault!' he shouted. 'You shouldn't have killed Pasha and taken Cush—'

He cringed as Tin Nose lifted his sword high above his head, but then saw Tin Nose pause as he noticed how trustingly Cush nestled in his arms. Slowly the sword went back to Tin Nose's side.

'Can you fix the creature's wing, boy?' he demanded gruffly. 'A flying bear that does not fly will be no use to the Witch's daughter and may cost me dear.'

'I can tie it up if you give me the things I need,' said Temmi coldly. 'And I do it for Cush, *not for you.*'

Tin Nose had some men bring strips of blanket for bandages and sent others to find twigs for splints. He stood at a distance, arms folded, watching impatiently as Temmi gently closed Cush's damaged wing to his body and tied it into place.

Cush was very frightened until he realized that Temmi was trying to help him, and except for a whimper or two, lay perfectly still. Afterwards, when Temmi was finished and both wings were bandaged tightly together, he shot Temmi a puzzled look.

'It's for your own good, Cush,' explained Temmi patting him.

Cush half-heartedly wagged his tail, not entirely convinced.

Tin Nose then ordered Temmi to put Cush back into his cage. Temmi hated doing this as much as he hated Tin Nose for ordering it, but he had no other choice.

Once the cage door was secured, Temmi found himself dragged across to one of the snow burrows and bundled inside it.

Tin Nose roared for Frostbite.

The wolf slunk across, low-bellied, casting his master sulky, simmering looks. Tin Nose grabbed his scruff and thrust him down beside Temmi, saying, 'If the brat tries to escape in the night, he is yours to swallow in as many bites as you please.'

Frostbite turned his head, his damp breath panting over Temmi's face.

'Rrrr . . . '

He showed every pointed tooth and fang; and Temmi wondered if this was how a wolf laughed.

* * *

29

It felt to Temmi as if he had only been asleep for a few minutes before he was awoken by movement and the sound of voices barking out orders. He opened his eyes and gazed out of the snow burrow. It was still completely dark, but the men were breaking up camp and the wolves were busily marking the place before moving on.

Temmi crawled out and ran across to peer into Cush's cage. The bear appeared utterly miserable, but otherwise no worse than yesterday.

Two unsmiling men approached, and ignoring Temmi's pleas to be careful, slotted a pair of poles through the cage and lifted it shoulder high. Cush turned restlessly, wondering how it was he was flying when his wings didn't beat.

'Don't worry, Cush. I'll walk alongside you,' whispered Temmi reassuringly.

Minutes later the party set off, with no sign of daylight in the sky and flurries of snow blowing into their eyes. It was the start of a long, difficult journey and always in snow: with it either heaped-up so deeply they had to dig through it, or thickening the air as a howling blizzard. And overshadowing them and stretching never-endingly into the distance, loomed ranks of nameless mountains, gale-blasted snow streaming from each shining peak like long powdery banners.

Temmi had seen mountains before but they were shadows compared to these. At night-time, when they made camp, he gazed up at them through the blue half-light and imagined he saw faces and shoulders and arms. In stories at the longhouse, he had heard that mountains were the bones of giants. But if these mountains *were* giants, they were far from dead, Temmi sure they were watching him all the time; and for their own cruel fun they sent avalanches thundering down, one great fall nearly sweeping them all away.

And if the snow and mountains were always present, so too was the bitter, bone-gnawing cold. Like the Witch's men, Temmi's skin gradually took on a grey colour: his lips turned grey and his eyes turned grey. His teeth no longer chattered, and he managed to get used to unfeeling feet and hands. And when he saw that his fingernails were black with cold, he shrugged and accepted this for the way things are in the High Witchlands. But really it was the cold which stopped him caring for everything—everything except Cush.

For much of the time, Temmi moved as if in a dream, frozen spindrift pulling at his heels and the endless snowy wastes emptying his thoughts, making him only aware of one foot going down after the other, stumbling into the deep boot-holes of the man who went before him. Even the wolves were less lively now, slinking along close beside the men, their coats weighed down with dirty ice. Without smells the land was as dead to them as it was for Temmi.

Then, ten days after they set out to reach it, they finally arrived at the Witch's castle. Despite his dullness, his sickness of all things snow and ice, Temmi lifted his head as if waking from a deep sleep, and stared in disbelief.

The castle was a jewel set in gardens of perfect snow, and was quite unlike any building he had ever seen before—or indeed, any building he had ever imagined possible. Like an iceberg it was built out of a single block of ice, yet was not rough and craggy as this might suggest; quite the opposite in fact. It was smooth and angular like a gigantic quartz crystal—with many leaning towers, as if an explosion of water had suddenly frozen. Yet it did not look like a castle, or a palace, or anywhere where people might live. There were no doors or windows that Temmi could see. There was nothing but massive crystal walls.

Arriving at its foot, they gathered before a deep ravine. Tin Nose immediately cupped his hands to his mouth and shouted above the droning wind, 'Lord Thurbolt commands you to open!'

At this, a slab of ice silently slid out from the base of the wall, crossing the ravine to form a bridge. At the same time a tall thin ice door opened above it, allowing the party to cross and enter.

Speechless with wonder, Temmi followed the others inside.

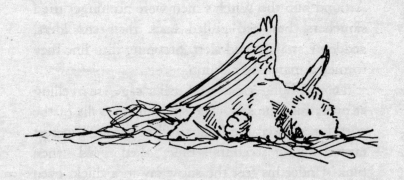

Chapter Six

When the ice door closed without a sound behind them, Temmi looked to see if he could find where it had been. But he could see no trace. The door had become part of the glassy wall once more. Around him the Witch's men were no longer tired slouchers, but had pulled back their shoulders, suddenly straight and alert. Stepping into line they formed a marching column.

Temmi hung close to Cush's cage, marvelling at everything he saw. The smooth ice walls of the corridor allowed the light to filter through in soft ever-changing colours—blue, then gold, then pink. Under his feet the snow lay in a thick, even carpet; and the ceiling was jagged with icicles.

If one were to fall, thought Temmi, it would pierce a man like a spear. Walking beneath such a ceiling was rather like entering a shark's mouth and waiting at any moment for it to snap shut.

Temmi (a little fish in such dangerous waters) lowered his head and Cush sniffed the air uneasily.

The corridor wound on and on, never once passing a door—or visible door—and never once coming upon another's footprints in the glittering snow. Presently they reached a grand staircase with columns of huge barley-sugar-twisted icicles and snowdrifts rising one upon another to form a delicate handrail.

At the top of the stairs, peering down at them, stood a thin woman in palest blue. She stood perfectly still, clutching her hands before her. Her silver hair was twisted into three cone-shaped horns on top of her head, and she wore icicle jewellery around her throat and wrists; long thin icicles hanging like needles from her ears. She looked as if she had been frozen to the spot; and Temmi shivered just to see her because her lips were blue and her skin was so white and utterly bloodless.

On reaching the top step, Tin Nose went forward, his lips brushing her cheek in a kiss. Her expression remained icy cold.

'Husband,' she murmured staring ahead into empty space.

'My Lady Sybia,' he replied. 'Are you well?'

She nodded slowly. 'In the best of cold health. But I fear the old Queen is failing fast. She asked for you to be brought to her as soon as you arrived.'

'Then take us to her at once.'

Lady Sybia turned and led them down an ice corridor, barely leaving a mark on the snow carpet, her light wispy gown floating about her. Watching her close to, Temmi realized that her lips and fingernails were not blue with paint and varnish, but from the bitter cold, and her jewellery gently tinkled as she moved, making the sound a chandelier makes when caught by a breeze.

Suddenly a wild shriek came from behind. The company halted and Lady Sybia frowned as a bare-footed girl, her hair as pointed as icicles, came racing up. The men immediately knelt, lowering their eyes and resting their heads against their spears.

'*Princess Agna,*' said Lady Sybia sternly, 'how many times do I have to tell you not to run? Running produces heat, and heat is the most hateful thing in the world.'

Princess Agna wasn't listening. 'Is that him? Is

that my flying bear?' she asked, jumping up and down and clapping her hands in delight. She made so much noise that Cush growled softly at her from the back of his cage.

'Tell it to be silent!' ordered the girl, her mouth suddenly becoming firm.

'If you stood still and stopped shouting,' said Temmi, 'Cush wouldn't growl so.'

Lady Sybia shot him a sharp glance and Princess Agna stood open-mouthed. Clearly nobody ever spoke to her in such a direct way.

'Tin Nose, why have you brought me another pet dwarf?' she cried, glancing across at Temmi. 'I've all the dwarfs I can play with already: and they're so bad-tempered and they don't wash and they always stink of their horrible pipe-tobacco. I don't want any more smelly old dwarfs.'

'Forgive me, Princess, he is not a dwarf,' replied Tin Nose respectfully. 'He is a boy.'

'A *boy*?' Princess Agna looked puzzled. 'Do you mean an ungrown man?'

'Yes, Princess. Unlike your dwarfs, this one will eventually grow to be as big as me.' His eyes met Temmi's. 'If he is lucky enough to live that long.'

'How tiresome and untidy. He will look out of place amongst my other dwarfs. Why did you bring him?'

37

'His services were needed, Princess. The flying bear was . . . *injured*. The boy takes care of it.'

Remembering the bear, Princess Agna grew excited once more. 'Take him from the cage and let me see him properly.'

'Do it, boy,' snarled Tin Nose.

Reluctantly Temmi opened the cage. 'Come on, Cush,' he whispered. 'Nobody will hurt you—not while *I'm* here.' He spoke these words just loud enough for the girl to hear.

Yet when she at last took Cush in her arms, Princess Agna held him clumsily, perhaps because she was not used to holding anything heavy—that after all was a servant's job. She squeezed him. The bear panicked and began to struggle. Stepping forward, Temmi quickly snatched him back and stroked him until he was calm again.

'The bear is bad-tempered and must be beaten!' announced the Princess. 'He must have his fur trimmed. It is making him too hot and irritable.'

Lady Sybia touched the Princess's shoulder with fingers as long and elegant as icicles. 'We can see to these matters later, Princess,' she said. 'But your royal mother first commands us to attend her.'

Temmi held Cush as they went on through the castle. The corridor grew higher and wider, with ice columns running down the middle and snow crisp upon the floor.

Then Lady Sybia stopped and reached out her hand, gently touching the frost-marbled wall with her fingertips. At once a huge slab of ice swung open and the company entered the Witch's chamber, wolves and all, their heads held low in respect for the dying Queen.

Temmi, at the back, felt uneasy. To be in the presence of a queen was one thing, but a queen who was also a witch! This gave him good reason to stand well back in the shadows—yet even from here he could not fail to notice the wintry splendour that surrounded him.

He saw that the Queen's bed was so large that it filled half the chamber: a solid block of softly glowing ice with a shining ice post at each corner. Draped from the posts were curtains of lace, made entirely of snowflakes, a criss-cross of delicate frosted strands woven together like the web of a snow spider. Behind them, Haggoth, Witch-Queen of the High Witchlands, appeared very old and frail. Her nose was long and pointed while the rest of her face was sunken and wrinkled. From her chin sprouted whiskers.

The men dropped to their knees and the wolves lay at the foot of her bed.

The Witch spoke.

'Lady Sybia . . . has your husband finally returned?'

Her voice sent a shiver through Temmi, not because it was frightening, but because it was so thin and brittle and *absolutely cold*.

Lady Sybia glided forward. 'Yes,' she breathed. 'He is here.'

'Tell him to step into the light so I may see him.'

Tin Nose obeyed, kneeling beside the bed. The Witch's claw of a hand reached out tremblingly until it rested on his head.

'You have returned safely, Lord Thurbolt. You have brought the flying bear and given it to Princess Agna?'

'Yes, Majesty.'

Haggoth sighed. 'Good. Then you have arrived in time for my death.'

'No!' screamed Princess Agna. 'I will not listen to such talk. You are a witch and can make yourself better. You will never die!'

As weak as she was, Haggoth turned to her with a terrible stare. 'Child—get rid of that melt water from your eyes or get out of my presence forever! You shall be a queen soon. Your heart must be ice. Always *ice*!'

The Princess took a deep breath and her tears, freezing on her face, dropped sparkling to the ground.

'She has much to learn,' sighed the Witch wearily. 'You and Lady Sybia must bring her up in my place, Thurbolt. You must teach her well. When she is twelve give her my wand and show her the magic of ice . . . the enchantment of snow . . . the bewitchment of frost. Make her love the Cold as much as I have, in all its cruelty and beauty.'

Tin Nose bowed low. 'I promise,' he said.

'And just as importantly, Thurbolt,' continued the Witch, her voice suddenly hardening, 'you must protect her from the evils of *warmth*. Warmth changes the unchangeable. It makes things that are solid melt away into nothing. It spoils the Great Whiteness and makes men weak—sitting stupidly around their fires idly watching the flames. It is the opposite of all we love and has a magic of its own, which we cannot control. Remember this, Thurbolt. Remember it always.'

'*Always*, Majesty.'

The claw lifted from his head. The Queen's eyes began to close. 'Go now. Leave me in peace to listen to the sweet murmuring of the ice.'

The men rose, bowed, and went out as silently as ghosts. The wolves crawled after them, their bellies touching the floor. At the door Temmi glanced back. The boot and pawprints were slowly disappearing from the snow, leaving it smooth and white once more.

The corridor seemed dazzling after the dimness of the Witch's bedchamber. The men led the wolves away to be fed. Lady Sybia turned to Princess Agna and with a cold smile said, 'Take your boy and bear to the nursery, Princess. I must speak with my husband.'

'Come on, boy,' said the Princess to Temmi. 'I will show you the dwarfs and where you will live.'

'Be sure not to run, Princess,' Lady Sybia called after her. 'You don't want to break out in an unhealthy pink flush.'

The Princess frowned. 'I shall do whatever I wish,' she muttered under her breath.

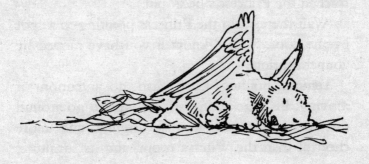

Chapter Seven

Princess Agna's nursery was in one of the many leaning towers, with walls and floors coming together at a sharp angle and the grain in the ice running in different directions. Most of the tower was taken up by crooked staircases and empty rooms, one leading into the next until at last they reached the Princess's bedroom.

'Wait there,' said the Princess pointing to a spot by the door. 'I shall know if you have moved by your footprints.'

Temmi, holding Cush, had no intention of moving; his gaze taking a long time to go around the room. He saw it was brighter and more cheerful than the Witch's room, and its furniture, all carved out of ice, was so odd that he nearly laughed out loud at it. For instance, the Princess's bed was a perfect snowdrift rather like a wave frozen before its foaming crest tumbles upon a beach. Instead of legs, the bed was held up by a number of snowmen standing shoulder to shoulder; a ladder held by a kneeling snowman the only way in, while getting out looked even more fun, judging by the number of slides Temmi counted.

Across, on the opposite side of the room, he saw the ice wall had been carved into deep shelves. On the shelves like living toys were the Princess's pet dwarfs. A couple sat playing cards, one chewed a long-stemmed pipe (not lit inside the palace, of course), another snoozed, and the last was carving a small block of ice into a frost flower.

Temmi stared, having never seen a dwarf before, because they weren't at all like small men. They were hairy, stocky creatures, with old men's faces. They had broad heads and tiny ears, wide mouths and small noses. Only one of them had a hairless chin.

They were also extremely noisy, squabbling about the cards, or being in each other's way; and they all elbowed the sleeper if he snored. Temmi thought they must enjoy squabbling because there were plenty of empty shelves where they could go to escape each other, only they seemed not to want to.

None of the dwarfs noticed them arrive until the Princess screamed at them to be silent.

They blinked down at her, screwing up their tiny eyes; their stares jumping from the girl to the boy to the bear in his arms.

'Come down,' ordered the Princess.

The dwarfs clumsily climbed off their shelf and came padding over. Temmi smiled once or twice at them, only to receive unfriendly scowls in return.

The girl introduced her pets. The bearded dwarfs were Wormlugs, Crumbtoot, Mudsniff, and Flywick. The beardless one was called Kobble. Temmi was introduced to them in passing as someone who looked after her bear.

'Begging pardon, Princess,' said Wormlugs, working up his shoulders. 'But he's not a proper dwarf. He's likely to grow lanky on you and try to boss us around.'

'Yes,' agreed Flywick. 'Big bosses little. That's the law of the world.'

'*I'm not a bully,*' said Temmi fiercely.

'It speaks!' cried Mudsniff amazed.

'But it's still not a proper dwarf,' grumbled

Wormlugs. 'Besides, there's no room for him on the shelves.'

Temmi saw this was clearly untrue, but said nothing. He did not like the idea of being somebody's pet and living on a shelf.

'The boy is my bear-keeper,' explained Princess Agna loftily. 'He and the bear must have a room of their own; and when the bear is well again he shall sleep at the bottom of my bed, and the boy can be given some other job at the palace—like ice polishing.'

This pleased the dwarfs no end and they nodded at each other, although Temmi was far less happy to hear his future so firmly decided for him.

'Now,' said the Princess moving on to other matters, 'if we don't soon play a game the day will be tiresome.'

'But what shall we play?' asked Flywick, trying to hide a bored yawn.

Kobble, the beardless dwarf, had an idea. 'What about dwarf skittles?' he suggested shyly. 'We haven't played that for ages.'

The four other dwarfs glared at him for daring to speak up.

'That is . . . ' said Kobble weakly, beginning to blush, 'if you feel that you . . . want to, Princess.'

The girl thought about it, her expression solemn. 'Yes,' she finally decided. '*Dwarf skittles*. I'd forgotten it was my favourite game and I order you to play it with me *now*.'

When she turned her back, the four other dwarfs pinched Kobble hard. Kobble pushed his fingers into his mouth to stop a cry coming out; and then Wormlugs glared at Temmi before pinching *him* for good measure too. It was as hard as the pinch he had given Kobble, right at the top of his arm.

Temmi learnt quickly what expert pinchers dwarfs can be.

The game of dwarf skittles was played along an ice-floored corridor. The rules were simple enough to be understood at a glance; in fact they were the same as in ordinary skittles, the only difference being that the wooden pins were replaced by living dwarfs, and the Princess took aim at their shins with a heavy wooden ball. When the ball hit a dwarf he was supposed to lie down. But dwarfs, as well as being first-rate pinchers, were also champion cheats and the world's worst losers. Temmi smiled as he watched them inch this way or that from the path of the ball, or simply deny it had touched them at all. The Princess screamed with rage, threatening all sorts of horrible tortures, but the dwarfs carried on as before.

'Such a hot-tempered one,' Wormlugs was heard to mutter into his beard and Princess Agna flared up again.

'Bad language! Bad language, Wormlugs! I shall tell Lady Sybia and she'll hang you by your thumbs from the roof of the wolf house.'

Temmi realized it was the word *hot* that had upset her so.

Mercifully a deep tolling bell put an end to all threats and squabbles.

'Good,' said Crumbtoot, patting his stomach. 'Dinner time. I'm starving.'

The dwarfs and the Princess hurried down to dinner in a noisy throng. Temmi followed holding a sleeping Cush; as he went along, Kobble sidled up and tugged at his coat. 'You mustn't mind us dwarfs,' he said when Temmi looked round at him. 'We're not really so bad once you get to know us.'

Temmi was not convinced. 'Do dwarfs always pinch so hard?' he asked.

'Oh yes,' replied Kobble proudly. 'As Wormlugs says, "Big bosses little, old bosses young". I'm the smallest and youngest dwarf, you see.'

'Huh, I suppose Wormlugs is the biggest and oldest?'

Kobble's face lit up with surprise. 'Why, yes. How did you guess?'

'It wasn't difficult.'

'But he's also the bravest too,' Kobble went on. 'He's always plotting things against Frostbite and working him up into a rage. They're deadly enemies, you see.' He glanced down at Cush peacefully asleep in Temmi's arms. 'Your bear looks much more friendly than any of the Witch's wolves. Do you think . . . that is . . . can I stroke—'

'Kobble!' snarled Wormlugs suddenly turning round and catching him. 'What have you to talk about with a *b-oy*? Come away to your own kind. He may be a spy.'

'I . . . I better go,' mumbled Kobble. 'Wormlugs is—'

'The biggest and the oldest,' finished Temmi sarcastically.

By this time they had entered the great hall, which lay at the very heart of the castle. Tables and benches were carved from ice and giant snowflakes hung from the domed ceiling like chandeliers. At the high table was a throne of clear ice—empty, of course, because the Witch-Queen was dying. On

50

one side of it sat Tin Nose, with Lady Sybia on the other. Princess Agna, Temmi, Cush, and the dwarfs crowded around the end of the table where manners were altogether more free and easy.

Below them sat the Witch's men, and the wolves were allowed to roam freely amongst them, finding food where they could.

'Here, doggie-doggie,' called Wormlugs, tossing Frostbite a bone—but when the wolf dived for it, Wormlugs reeled it in, laughing: the bone was tied to a piece of string.

'*Rarrr!*' Frostbite's yellow eyes glared at Wormlugs, full of deep hatred.

'One day, dwarf, you will torment my wolf once too often,' murmured Tin Nose calmly, 'and then you will wish you hadn't.' Meaningfully he tapped his false nose, which tonight was gold with a ruby set in the end—like an ugly boil, thought Temmi.

The food arrived with noise and clamour, and eagerly Temmi sat waiting for it, until he saw what it was—meat . . . blood-red meat, not the slightest bit cooked—and then he was nearly sick. How much better it had been even on the long journey there, with fish every night, cooked over the camp fire. This was not Tin Nose showing him any kindness. Not at all: Tin Nose realized that a flying bear needs fish, so Temmi was allowed to catch it for him and the extra ones he kept for himself. And Temmi had eaten well and often, while here at the Witch's table he would rather starve.

The meal started and Temmi quickly decided that perhaps worse than the food itself was having to watch others who considered it delicious. In open-mouthed horror he saw Princess Agna seize the meat in her neat little hands and begin taking savage bites. Soon her face and fingers were red and sticky with blood. And finally done, she carelessly tossed the picked bone away to the wolves, only to snatch another raw steak from the pile.

'Don't you want any?' she asked Temmi through gnawing bites.

'No, Princess,' he muttered weakly. 'You can have my share if you like.'

Then a dish of uncooked vegetables was slammed down and the waiting dwarfs pounced upon it. In the scramble a hunk of swede rolled Temmi's way and he snatched it up and gobbled it down. However, when he tried to take something else from the dish, Wormlugs deliberately blocked him with his back. Noticing this, Kobble gave Temmi a carrot, passing it to him under the table. Yet no sooner was it in Temmi's hand than Wormlugs snatched it back.

Temmi was so angry at this that he let it be known in a way the dwarf best understood—with a sharp pinch right between his shoulder blades. Wormlugs gave an unnecessarily loud howl and leapt to his feet.

'Dwarf-slayer!' he bawled.

'Thief!' returned Temmi.

Seconds later fists were flying, sending plates and dishes clattering to the floor. Hardly had the fight begun than Tin Nose rushed over and tore the two apart. The whole hall was silent and watching.

'Such behaviour before a princess,' hissed Lady Sybia. 'Mark my words, husband, that boy will bring nothing but trouble.'

Tin Nose drew his sword.

'Put that away, Tin Nose!' ordered Princess Agna, her face as bloody as a feeding tiger's and her eyes blazing.

Tin Nose hesitated. 'One day soon, Princess, you will be Queen,' he said in a soft purring growl. 'You should remember to keep about you only those whose presence is fit.'

'And *you* should remember that when *I* am Queen *I* shall give the commands, not *you*, Tin Nose.'

The Princess took another slab of meat and

without turning her head ordered the guards to take the two fighters from the table. 'Let them go hungry. That shall be their punishment,' she said.

Temmi was glad it was left to her to decide, for as he and Wormlugs were marched away he caught the look on Tin Nose's face as reluctantly he re-sheathed his sword.

Chapter Eight

That night Temmi lay shivering under a greasy wolf skin on the floor of his ice cell next to the Princess's bedroom. He was unable to sleep, and cold and hunger made him even more miserable. Despite trying not to he kept thinking about his father and his old home by the lake. His thoughts became so real that he imagined he could smell freshly-caught fish baking in the fire and warm bread, crusty and good. Tear followed tear down his cheeks until Cush's fur grew damp where Temmi rested his head.

All around them the castle was still. *Still* but not silent, for the ice softly creaked and groaned under its own great weight, speaking the secret language of ice.

But then, as Temmi listened, he heard the unmistakable sound of a door opening. It was the door to the Princess's bedroom; and judging by the great care being taken, he was not supposed to hear it at all. Voices whispered. Cush stirred.

'Hush,' Temmi whispered to him. 'It's those sneaky dwarfs.'

Temmi and Cush listened carefully, wondering what was going on. At first Temmi thought that Wormlugs had bullied the other dwarfs into ganging up on him, to get his revenge. But he quickly realized this wasn't so: if anything, the dwarfs were taking extra care to stay well away from him, creeping by on some other secret business of their own.

The snow crunched ever so slightly beneath the dwarfs' sealskin boots, but most noise was made by Wormlugs telling his fellows to be quiet.

Reaching the far wall they pushed open the door and crept out into the passageway. Then the door swished shut behind them.

Curious, Temmi jumped up; Cush bounded up with him, but Temmi shook his head. 'No, Cush. You stay here—you can stand guard.'

Cush yawned. It was obvious he'd be asleep in a minute or two. Temmi gave him a friendly pat and left.

Following the dwarfs' footprints, Temmi found the hidden door. He saw everything perfectly clearly even without a light, for moonlight streamed through the ice castle making the walls shimmer a ghostly blue.

Temmi pushed open the door and peered through. The passageway outside was empty and the dwarfs' footprints were fast fading in the snow. Quickly he hurried after them. The footprints ended abruptly at a blank wall. Temmi touched it and a door opened for him. Behind it lay, not another empty chamber as he expected, but a circular stairway going down as deeply as a well.

If Temmi hesitated it was only for a moment, then he started the downward climb, determined to discover the dwarfs' secret. The stairs went on twisting beneath him, and almost without him noticing, the ice turned into rock—then the light changed. No longer was it blue powdery moonlight, but flickering orange firelight; and while the moonlight had come down from above, the orange firelight sprang up from below.

Knowing he was close to finding his answer, Temmi cautiously approached the light which moved restlessly across the wet rock—now red, now yellow, now orange. Besides the light there was also smoke—wood-smoke—rising up the stairs like a chimney; and Temmi could hear sticks crackling as they burned. Then, catching low voices, he stood listening to the dwarfs talking amongst themselves around their fire.

'Ahh, this is the warmest my toes have been all day,' he heard Mudsniff sigh contentedly. 'I'm sure my beard has frozen stiff. It feels as if I could snap it off my chin like an icicle.'

'You'd look as stupid as Kobble if you did,' said Crumbtoot.

Gruff dwarfish laughter broke out at this.

Peering around the bottom of the stairway, Temmi saw a good fire burning well, sending up sparks to the roof of a cave. The dwarfs sat close to the flames, their faces shining in the fierce orange light.

As he carried on watching, Temmi saw Wormlugs take up a shovel which had been roughly hammered into a frying-pan shape. This set the other dwarfs busily emptying their pockets, taking out pieces of raw meat that they had stolen at dinner time and arranging them carefully in the pan for frying.

'Oldest and biggest gets bestest and mostest,' declared Wormlugs greedily.

'Why are your pieces of meat always covered in fluff, Kobble?' complained Flywick.

'Give him a good pinch,' said Wormlugs. 'That'll wake his ideas.'

'*You leave him be!*' cried Temmi, suddenly stepping out from the shadows.

The dwarfs froze in surprise. In fact at that moment they looked exactly like gargoyles, and their open mouths might have been made that way for spouting rainwater. Had he not been so angry with them, Temmi probably would have laughed out loud—but he was not in the mood for laughing at anything just then.

'*Kobble is the only good one amongst you,*' he shouted. 'None of you other dwarfs would share your food with me. *You'd let me starve!*'

Wormlugs picked up the frying pan, which he had dropped into the flames when Temmi first appeared. The hot handle made him grimace.

'Told you he was the Witch's spy,' he said darkly. 'That pipsqueak, that halfling, that *pretend* dwarf.'

Kobble began to snivel, then Flywick started to cry, setting off Crumbtoot and Mudsniff. Wormlugs fought against it, but he was pretty near to weeping himself and kept clearing his throat unconvincingly.

'Why are you crying?' asked Temmi surprised.

'*Because you will tell the Witch*,' wailed Mudsniff, '*and she will nail our beards to the trees and leave us there for the crows.*'

Ignoring the fact that Kobble had no beard to be hung up by, Temmi said, 'Tell her what?'

'Th-that we have l-lit a f-fire at the pa-palace; and to w-warm yourself by f-fire and to eat h-hot dinners are b-both a-gainst the l-law.'

'Against the law?'

'Punishable by death,' whispered Flywick.

Temmi paused to consider the number of times he must have broken the Witch's law. 'Well, I shan't tell her. Move up. Give me some room. Don't you think I hate being cold too?'

They stared at him in astonishment.

'I suppose we could make room,' said Crumbtoot slowly.

'And if you're cooking, I wouldn't mind a share of the meat,' said Temmi peering into the pan. 'Well fried, please—all the way through.'

Now they weren't going to be hung up and left for the crows, the dwarfs' mood quickly changed. 'Boys are pretty much like dwarfs,' decided Kobble happily.

'Pretty much,' agreed Temmi.

The dwarfs threw more sticks on the fire and

the hot pan made the meat sizzle in its own juices, the smell growing more and more delicious until the meat was cooked and ready to be eaten.

They had no plates, but the flat stones scattered about the cave did just as well; and Wormlugs was content to eat straight from the pan. Nobody spoke as they chewed, it was understood to be too serious a business to interrupt with idle chit-chat. The older dwarfs used their beards as napkins; Kobble and Temmi licked their fingers clean. Not a bit was wasted.

It was while they were finishing their supper that a bell began to toll, sounding loudly even deep underground.

Straight away Wormlugs leapt to his feet, his eyes slitted and suspicious.

'The warning bell!' he cried. 'The boy *is* a spy after all. He's betrayed us to the Witch!'

'No,' insisted Flywick. 'Why ring the bell when we might easily be arrested without half so much fuss? This is something bigger than dwarfs warming their beards by the fire.'

'Perhaps the castle is under attack,' suggested Kobble.

'*Stupid*—who'd dare attack the Witch?' growled Wormlugs giving him a sly pinch.

Temmi chewed his lip. 'Then there is only one possible answer,' he said gravely. 'The Witch . . . she's finally died.'

And they all looked at each other in wonder.

Chapter Nine

By moonlight they carried the Witch's frail body
out of the castle on a slab of ice: a servant at each
corner and one at each side. The Witch was
dressed in sparkling white like a bride on her
wedding day, a smile upon her face because she
had found the most lasting cold of all.

Behind the Witch came her people and her
wolves, passing between shapeless heaps of snow.

At the front, the most important mourners were
also dressed in purest white—Lady Sybia's veil
reaching her knees; her blue lips the only part of
her face to be seen through it. Her husband, Tin
Nose, wore his best ermine-trimmed coat, and his
silver nose had flaring nostrils that coiled back in

deep grooves. Beside him Princess Agna sobbed bitterly.

'*Control*, madam! *Control!*' Lady Sybia hissed at her from beneath her veil.

Further down the line, where the mourners wore simple white ribbons, the dwarfs were to be found; but Temmi and Cush were right at the back among the lame and grizzled old wolves, surrounded by pot scourers and ice polishers, strange misshapen creatures who shuffled along in sacking tied up with string.

In the silence, Temmi caught snatches of their fearful whispers.

'What will it be like having a girl rule over us?' hissed a voice at his side.

'Not a girl,' answered another voice, 'she is too young. The power will be in Lord Thurbolt's hands, at least until the Princess is older.'

'But what if he gets a taste for power?'

'Hush, that is not our business. Let us see off the old Queen first.'

Handfuls of snow came on the wind, flecking hair and the wolves' ragged coats. A blizzard was stirring itself, some saying it was right and proper that it should; others murmuring that it was the Witch's last gasp of magic. Nobody thought to hurry because of it; and at a stately pace they carried the Witch down to the river where her dragon boat had waited since the day she first fell ill.

Carefully the slab-carriers laid the Witch upon the deck before solemnly filing back across the gangplank. With his sword Tin Nose hacked through the mooring rope and the sail came down with a sound like a rug being shaken, revealing the Witch's symbol—the black snowflake that a thousand suns cannot melt.

Then, with everyone gathered to watch, the boat was caught by the current and moved smoothly away from the bank, out into the middle of the river.

The sight sent Agna mad with grief. She would have thrown herself into the water after it had not Tin Nose grabbed her and pulled her back.

Pulling free of his grasp she scrambled away, the wolves streaming after her; and all through the night they ran wild together, howling and raging at the moon.

Chapter Ten

'The Queen is dead: long live the Queen!'

This was a cry Temmi heard many times over the next few days. He started singing it to Cush, and Cush, not knowing what it meant, simply wagged his tail affectionately.

But a great change had begun with Haggoth, the old Queen, dying.

Returning to the castle at dawn, Agna amazed all the people she met by how calm and sure of herself she now was. Those who saw her reported that although her eyes were red she no longer cried, her tears having all turned to ice. Beside her the wolves walked respectfully, and along the passageways her men dropped to their knees, lowering their gaze.

She never returned to the nursery. Her dwarfs and other toys lay forgotten. Temmi heard she had taken over the rooms in the old Queen's part of the castle; and after that he saw her only in the great hall during feasts or at meal times, dining on tiny scraps of raw meat. And if he looked too hard towards the high throne his eyes were dazzled by her frost crown. It was as if she had given herself over completely to the Cold, which naturally thrilled Lord Thurbolt and his wife.

'Majesty,' breathed Lady Sybia curtsying low, 'it chills my heart with gladness to see you make yourself so like your dear mother.'

Agna stared at her coldly. '*Her* law is *my* law. The ice shall not give an inch to the thaw. Serve me and see it is so.'

Lady Sybia trembled with pleasure. She was sure Agna would make a great queen, perhaps even greater than her mother.

The dwarfs quickly grew bored. They were so used to being pets of a princess that without their mistress they couldn't organize themselves to do anything except squabble: Wormlugs starting an argument if ever they needed one (which usually they didn't), while poor Kobble was pinched into silence the moment he opened his mouth. Quite honestly Temmi lost patience with them.

He much preferred to spend his time with Cush. Cush didn't argue about who had the most eyelashes, or who was able to hold his breath the longest, or who woke up first that morning. Cush was better company by far; and if his injured wing meant he was still unable to fly, well, Temmi was happy just having the little bear gambolling along beside him.

Each day, at some point, Temmi made sure he took Cush up on the castle roof. The visit was worthwhile for the view alone, with towers sprouting out below and shooting up behind like frozen rockets—and beyond lay the snowfields and the forest, stretching as far as the mountains themselves. But there was another, more serious reason behind their visits.

Temmi knew that Cush had to learn the different winds that blew—because to a flying bear these are as important as ocean currents are to whales and dolphins; each wind as distinct as the colours of the rainbow. The north wind was black, the south wind yellowy-green, the east wind blue, and the west wind brown with orange tips; and the winds in between were shades of all the others.

One day, as Cush's wet, sniffly nose was learning all about a purply-grey north-westerly, a voice spoke to Temmi.

He spun round and there was Agna. She was standing on a slightly higher roof, barefoot in the snow. For a moment Temmi forgot she was Queen of the High Witchlands and saw only a small girl dressed in clothes that didn't quite fit her, as if they were the clothes of a grown-up. But then he remembered who she had become and bowed low, allowing Cush to jump up into his arms. The cub didn't know whether to growl or wag his tail.

Agna stared at him. 'The bear—doesn't he fly yet?'

Temmi gave Cush a gentle stroke. 'No, Majesty. His wing needs a little more time.'

'Oh.' Agna made an empty sound and glanced about her as if never really interested in the first place.

'But he is getting stronger, thank you, Majesty.'

'Oh?'

'And eating more fish.'

'Indeed?'

'Soon I hope he will be flying again.'

'Yes.'

'Would . . . would you like to stroke him, Majesty?'

'*No* . . . no thank you.'

An awkward silence fell between them. Temmi smiled. He half expected Agna to burst out laughing at any moment and give up this grand pretence.

But Agna only tilted her head and looked at him, puzzled. 'Why do you smile?'

'Oh, nothing, Majesty. I was just thinking: Cush and I are often here, but we have never before seen you on the roofs.'

'That is because I have been exploring,' she said airily. 'It is my first task as Queen to find every room in my castle, then it has no secrets to use against me.' Suddenly her voice grew low and confiding. 'But listen, Temmi, I have seen so many things you wouldn't believe. Only this morning I . . . Oh, but naturally I can't tell you—I am Queen, you understand, and such sights are for the Queen's eyes only.'

Temmi thought she had almost forgotten about the crown upon her head and become just an ordinary girl bursting to tell her news. He was right. Agna longed to tell him about the room that held the skin of a frost dragon, and the room with thousands of brightly jewelled fish frozen

71

into the walls. Then there was the room where the yellow ice was more ancient than the land, and the room with more ways in than out, which held the old Witch's three great books of magic: one that governed the snow, one that governed the frost, and one that governed the ice.

'I'm sure you do the right thing, Majesty,' replied Temmi, who couldn't resist adding, 'Why, the mysteries of the castle aren't for the likes of a humble bear-keeper and poor fisherman's son.'

He thought she would recognize the gentle teasing and manage a smile—if only a little one. But when he looked across he saw Agna wasn't paying him the slightest attention.

'What's that noise?' she demanded.

Becoming once more royal and aloof, she moved closer to the edge and peered down. Temmi, holding Cush, followed but kept a pace behind. Below them on the snow plains he saw the five dwarfs returning from the forest. And the thought of a warm fire built from the wood they had gathered had put them in such a good mood that they were less quarrelsome and better tempered than usual. As Agna and Temmi watched, they laughed at Kobble as he threw himself into the snow—and it was their undignified honks, howls, and hee-haws that Agna had heard.

Temmi grew worried. Hadn't he warned Wormlugs to take more care? Before, when they had a princess to amuse, the dwarfs made do by smuggling in a few twigs at a time. But lately, with no one to question their comings and goings, they'd become dangerously careless about what they did, even now dragging a heavy log behind them.

'Why do they laugh?' asked Agna irritably. 'Don't they know laughter is a weakness that comes from unnecessary feelings of warmth?'

Temmi thought, you're just saying the words that Tin Nose and his wife put into your head, but he said, 'Oh, you know how the dwarfs are, Majesty. Did you hear of Wormlugs's latest trick he played on Lord Thurbolt's wolf? Oh—and I nearly forgot to tell you, Cush has learnt to walk on his back legs, shall I sh—'

'And why are they bringing that filthy log into my castle? What can they possibly want it for?'

Before Temmi could think up a good reason, she murmured to herself, 'If those dwarfs are up to any mischief, I shall find out. The castle has no secrets from its Queen.'

In their cave deep beneath the cellars of the ice castle, the dwarfs kept adding to their store of firewood, heaping it higher. Rarely, if ever, did they allow the fire to go out now, and if it grew low they quickly built it up again with twigs and logs. They spent many hours around it, hating the times they had to leave and go out into the cold.

Temmi did his best, he tried to warn them of the risk they took: but even he was drawn to the warmth of the fireside more often than he should have been.

And so it was that they were all gathered there, spreading their hands to the flames, when Queen Agna came down the twisting stairway and caught them.

'*How dare you!*' she screamed. 'How dare you bring this *evil* into the house of the Witch-Queen? You shall pay for this outrage—every one of you! You shall pay with your lives!'

The dwarfs immediately fell to their knees, whimpering and moaning and begging for mercy. Temmi, however, grew angry. Before him was no queen in a rage, but a girl—a rather small girl—in a tantrum.

'How can you be so afraid?' he cried, turning to the dwarfs; and determined to show them that what he saw was the truer picture, he ran over, grabbed Agna's ice cold wrist and dragged her towards the fire.

'What are you doing?' she shrieked. 'Take your hands off me this minute. I am your Queen and I order you not to touch me!'

'Oh, be quiet you . . . you . . . great spoilt baby!' blurted out Temmi, shocking the dwarfs as much as Agna.

'What can you be thinking of, boy?' hissed Wormlugs. 'You'll only make matters worse for us all. You'll only make our deaths more terrible.'

But Temmi was in no mood to listen. He shoved Agna down onto one of the large stones they used as seats and stepped back so she could feel the fire's strength.

'Torture! Torture!' she screamed. The dwarfs covered their ears and rolled into balls like hedgehogs.

'Of course it's not torture,' sneered Temmi. 'You only believe that because you were told it was true. Learn for yourself. The fire's warmth is actually kind.'

'I'm dying—you're killing me,' she cried, although she was struggling less and less. 'See, I shake all over—I have caught a deadly disease.'

Temmi smiled. 'It is called shivering,' he explained patiently, as if to a very young child. 'And you're shivering because you've never realized just exactly how cold you were before.'

Agna fell silent. Soon she stopped shivering; she reached out her hands to the fire, a growing look of wonder on her face.

'Ah—ah, not too close,' warned Temmi, 'or the flames really *will* hurt you.'

At their feet the dwarfs slowly uncurled and sat up, staring at Agna in utter bewilderment. A rosiness was just appearing in the girl's cheeks, making her look less severe—and some might say pleasant.

Kobble smiled at the change. But when Agna tried a warm smile back at him, she was unsure which way her mouth should move (it is something others do without thinking, but she would have to learn).

As her body thawed, so did her thoughts. She began to remember a time and place outside the ice castle. But it was all so confusing—frightening too: her mind spinning with colours and the echo of distant voices.

Suddenly and firmly her duty to the Cold blocked out these things and she snatched back her hands.

'*What am I doing?*' she cried in disbelief. 'The frost crown is melting!' And she fled to the stairs, scrambling up them, the crown crooked and misshapen upon her head.

The dwarfs watched her go with gasps of dismay.

'Now she will surely send for the guards and they will kill us,' groaned Mudsniff.

'I don't think so,' said Temmi confidently, reaching out to the flames once more. 'If they kill us for breaking the law they must also kill the Queen. After all, hasn't she just warmed herself before our fire?'

The dwarfs knew this was true. The law was greater than any one person—even the Queen.

Wormlugs chuckled softly, and giving the boy an admiring look, said, 'Oh, you're a crafty one all right.'

Chapter Eleven

As the lives of dwarfs and humans took their
many twists and turns, Cush seemed to improve
by the day. New feathers grew where the damaged
ones had been, while his injured wing mended so
well that Temmi no longer saw a need to bandage
it, encouraging the bear to use both wings as
much as possible. Unfortunately, Cush had become
so used to living among creatures who stayed
firmly on the ground, that he forgot he could fly.
The only answer, Temmi realized, was to teach
him.

After that, it became a common sight to see
Temmi take the bear out of the castle for his daily
flying lessons. Of course, had Pasha been alive she

would have done as much herself, the only difference being that Pasha would have been teaching her cub something she knew, while Temmi, who flapped his arms madly until they ached, only managed to make himself look foolish. The trouble was, Cush had become lazy, and every time Temmi threw him up into the air he simply glided back to earth . . . and stayed there. It was *so* frustrating.

'Cush! You have turned into a floppy old sag bear,' Temmi would shout at him at the end of each lesson.

Cush's reply, as always, was to hang out his tongue and pant happily.

In the end Temmi asked the dwarfs to help him. They grumbled but agreed. Now, whenever Cush was in the air, they simply refused to let him land, clapping their hands and shooing him back into the sky. It made quite a funny sight, with dwarfs running into each other or suddenly blundering waist-deep into snow.

By and by Cush realized he *was* a flying bear after all and took great delight in the fact, never again walking if he could use his wings instead. Even in the castle he constantly buzzed around Temmi's head, nuzzling his neck or licking his face.

But the more pleased with himself Cush became, the more gloomy was Temmi.

He reached up and tickled Cush's belly. 'You don't deserve to be a prisoner here, Cush,' he said softly. 'One day when you are big and strong I promise I will let you go free.' He blinked back a tear. 'As for me, I will probably end my days as an ice polisher—a slave of the Witch-Queen for ever.'

Fish.

That was the other great thing in their lives.

Fish.

No sooner was Cush flying again than he seemed to be hungry all the time. He awoke in the night yowling for fish, and if Temmi had none to give him he covered his head with a wing and sulked. Yet it was rare for Cush to go hungry for long, and the nursery floor was soon so littered with fish heads and bones that even Wormlugs complained of the stink.

Once, maybe twice a day, Temmi took Cush to the river to hunt, the sight never failing to thrill him. First, the long dive with wing tips nearly touching—then the smallest of splashes—speedily followed by the graceful climb back into the sky, a trout squirming between Cush's front paws. Often Temmi put out a fishing line of his own, but the river was so full of fish that, as a fisherman's son, he found them almost embarrassingly easy to catch (not that anyone else fished there: back at the castle, the river and the things that lived in it were considered unlucky).

Returning home one day with a catch so heavy it had to be dragged behind on a string (each fish tail chewed ragged by Cush), Temmi spied Tin Nose and his wife talking together on the forest track.

Tin Nose had pulled up on a sleigh roped to four pairs of wolves, Frostbite their front runner. Lady Sybia sat side-saddle on a white elk.

'What can they be up to so far away from the castle?' wondered Temmi, suddenly curious to find out.

He beckoned Cush down into his arms and crept through the trees until he reached a snowdrift where he could hide and listen.

'Well, tell me what exactly these worries are,' he heard Tin Nose demand.

Lady Sybia slowly wound the reins around her cold, bloodless hands. 'They are mostly feelings, husband, but I do truly believe our Queen is no longer of the Cold.'

'This is serious, lady. You need evidence for what you say.'

Lady Sybia kept her gaze firmly fixed on the sparkling frost fire of her rings. 'Very well . . . She has demanded extra furs on her bed and dresses indecently warm. She plays with her food at the table and has recently asked me whether meat would not taste better *cooked*.'

'What did you tell her?'

She glared up at him. 'The truth of course! That cooked meat is poisonous.'

'Is there anything else?' asked Tin Nose gravely.

'Yes . . . Have you noticed her skin is no longer the healthy white it once was? And yesterday— *yesterday* I caught her rubbing her hands together.'

'Did you not ask her why?'

'Of course,' snapped his wife. 'She said she had an itch. Even if this were true she should be so sweetly numb with cold that such an irritation would pass unnoticed. But I do genuinely believe she was . . . she was rubbing her hands together for *warmth*.'

Tin Nose breathed out through a nose rather like a wolf's snout.

'Others are beginning to notice these things too,' went on his wife. 'There is talk about the

82

castle. I tell you she has broken faith with the Cold. This will end in thaw and death.'

'You go too fast!' cried Tin Nose. 'What about my promise to the old Witch? I gave my word I would turn the girl into a fitting queen.'

'I say Haggoth was wrong to expect such a thing. After all, the girl is not even of royal blood.'

Tin Nose glanced about. 'Speak lower, lady. Nobody but us knows she is adopted and not born to the throne, not even the girl herself.'

'Then, Thurbolt, perhaps it is time they did. It is now clear to me she is unfit to rule and always has been. The warning signs were there to see. Remember how easily she cried? And you can never make an icicle out of salt water.'

Tin Nose turned to her sharply. 'What is it you want me to do?'

'She must be removed.'

'But she is the Queen.'

'She has broken the law.'

'But who will replace her?'

Lady Sybia touched his shoulder. 'Why *us*, husband. Who is more loyal to the Cold than Lord Thurbolt and his wife? And the wolves respect you.'

Tin Nose gave a snort, unhappy at the idea.

'Won't gossips say we did away with the new Queen to keep the crown for ourselves?'

Lady Sybia smiled, or rather her numbed blue lips formed the shape of a smile, for there was not a spark of warmth in it.

'They will not be able to if they believe it was the work of another.'

Tin Nose frowned. 'Who?'

'The boy. The one with the bear. He's a person of no importance at the castle and has already shown he has a violently hot temper. What a perfect gift he is to us.'

'And when shall it be done?'

'As soon as possible. *Tonight*, when the traitor is asleep in her nice *warm* bed.'

'Very well,' agreed Tin Nose slowly. 'You have convinced me, lady. I will do it.'

'You will not be sorry,' she murmured.

Just then, as she spoke, the breeze changed direction, carrying a strange new smell to the wolves, a mixture of boy, bear, and fish. Growls and snarls broke out along the line.

'Someone must be coming,' said Lady Sybia urgently. 'We should not be seen acting suspiciously together. *Go*, husband.'

Tin Nose cracked his whip. The wolves obediently set off, low and sleek, the runners of his sleigh cutting the snow like knives. Lady Sybia turned her white elk around and kicked her heels. The elk half reared, then dashed straight for the snowdrift where Temmi lay.

Temmi hid his face in Cush's fur, listening as the creature's hooves galloped ever nearer. Then there was a silence as it cleared both him and the drift in a single leap, landed, and went on its way without Lady Sybia noticing he was there.

For a long time Temmi didn't dare move. He held Cush tightly, trying to take in what he had heard. The worst part was knowing this was all his fault, for wasn't he the one who had forced Agna to understand about fire and warmth? And now, because of that, she was going to be killed.

'We can't let this happen, Cush,' he whispered. 'We just can't.'

Suddenly he jumped up and raced towards the castle, tripping and falling in his haste.

Above him circled Cush who searched the horizon for wolves. There *must* be wolves. Why else would the boy be in such a panic?

Chapter Twelve

First Temmi ran to find the dwarfs. As usual they were warming themselves by the fire in their secret cave—and also as usual they were squabbling.

'I'm the oldest and biggest,' Wormlugs was shouting, prodding his chest with a finger. 'I should know.' (They were arguing over which of two cockroaches had the longest legs.)

'Oldest and biggest doesn't always mean rightest,' said Kobble innocently. For that he was given a firm pinch.

'Oh . . . I stand corrected,' he muttered.

'Stop bickering and listen to me!' cried Temmi suddenly bursting in.

They turned to him in surprise.

'I have just overheard Tin Nose and Lady Sybia plotting to kill the Queen,' said Temmi. 'They're going to do it tonight when she is asleep, and tomorrow they will rule the High Witchlands in her place.'

Wormlugs sniffed and shrugged. 'Nothing to do with the dwarfs,' he said dismissively. 'Big matters pass over the heads of little men.'

'But don't you see, this is all our doing. They have guessed Agna has betrayed the Cold, and it was us and our fire that did it. We must do something to help her. We can't just stand by and let Tin Nose get away with it!'

The dwarfs looked at each other, unsure, managing not to meet Temmi's eye. But suddenly Kobble jumped up. 'I agree with Temmi,' he said bravely; and seeing Wormlugs angrily twitching his fingers, pinched himself before the bigger dwarf had the chance to.

Wormlugs was still not convinced, so Temmi said, 'Do you think you can live safely with Tin Nose your king? What if he remembers how badly you've treated his favourite wolf and decides to have you thrown to Frostbite just for the fun of it? *Think*, Wormlugs, what other use can he have for dwarfs?'

'Hmm . . . ' Wormlugs thoughtfully chewed

the end of his beard. 'I believe the boy may have a point. But what can we do?'

'We must go to Agna when she is alone and warn her.'

'We can do it when she is in her chamber last thing tonight,' suggested Crumbtoot.

Temmi nodded. 'Yes, and we must be sure to get there before Tin Nose and his crafty wife.'

Night came quickly to the northern lands, but the moon took its time to appear. Rising slowly over the mountains, its beams touched the ice castle and it gleamed all at once and magically—like a milky gemstone.

It was time to go. Temmi and the dwarfs crept out of the nursery, Cush with them, making himself known with a ghostly flutter of his wings. The passageway stretched into the distance and before them a billion crystals glinted in the snow carpet.

The dwarfs were extremely jumpy. 'We shall hang by our beards for this,' Mudsniff kept muttering.

'If we do they're sure to hang me first,' growled Wormlugs, 'because I'm the oldest and biggest.'

'No they won't,' said Flywick.

Temmi shook his head in despair. Even at a time like this they still managed to argue.

They moved through the castle without meeting another soul, until at last they came to the Queen's room. The dwarfs elbowed Temmi to the front and he touched the door with his fingertips. Slowly it swung open.

Agna was sitting on the edge of her bed looking rather bored and lost in the velvety folds of an ermine cloak, which she had pulled up close about her. As the door opened she guiltily threw it off and jumped up. Seeing Temmi and Cush and her dear funny old dwarfs she smiled briefly in delight, but then remembering she was now Queen, her hands went to her hips and her expression turned proud.

'How dare you burst—'

'Majesty,' said Temmi calmly, 'there is no time. We have come to warn you of a plot to take your life.' And he quickly told her what he'd overheard from Tin Nose and his wife.

Agna sat very still as she listened, stroking Cush who was curled up in her lap. Afterwards she smiled in disbelief.

'They wouldn't dare raise a hand against me,' she said. 'You are wrong.'

'They think you have broken faith with the

Cold,' said Temmi, adding quietly, 'And it's true—you have.'

Agna shrugged. 'I am Queen. Tin Nose made a promise to my mother, the Witch. He would never break his word, not to her.'

'*But that's just it*,' cried Temmi. 'The Witch *isn't* your mother—at least not your proper one. You are her adopted daughter, only she never told you. I heard Tin Nose say so.'

Briefly the flash of friendly faces and the echo of voices returned to Agna.

'No, I don't believe you,' she said, trying to forget them and clear her head. 'It's not possible, these are just lies.'

'At least give us the chance to prove it to you,' said Temmi.

'How?'

'If you agree to hide yourself, we will make your bed appear as if you were still in it, fast asleep. Then in the morning we'll come back and see if anything has happened.'

'Very well,' agreed Agna. 'But I don't expect to find it has.'

The dwarfs, working together, scooped up snow from the floor and arranged it in a heap upon the bed. Then Mudsniff carefully draped the ermine cloak over it. To anyone not in on the secret, there was no reason to believe it was not the Queen asleep in her bed.

'And just where do you plan to hide me?' asked Agna as they led her away.

'In our secret place. But don't worry,' Temmi quickly assured her, 'we shall put out the fire as soon as we get there.'

'No . . . please don't,' murmured Agna. 'I have dreamt about fire ever since you first showed it to me, and I long to be warm again.'

'As your Majesty demands,' said Wormlugs with a sly smile, 'so shall it be.'

They kept themselves warm through the dark night; Temmi frying his fish in the frying pan and Agna tasting cooked food for the first time, eating greedily when she discovered how good it was. Then, in the early hours, they crept back to her room, wondering what they would find.

The door swished open. Eyes peered inside—gazing in silent horror at what they saw. Through the ermine cloak and carefully arranged snow, into the ice bed itself, was thrust an ugly twisted icicle.

There could be no doubt in Agna's mind now.

Angrily she clenched her hands. 'I will have Tin Nose and his wife arrested and dragged through the castle in chains for this!'

But as she spoke, a distant voice arose. 'The traitor Queen is dead! Long live their Majesties Thurbolt and Sybia—and may the Cold be unending.'

'They have outflanked you,' said Crumbtoot slowly.

'We shall hang by our beards,' groaned Mudsniff.

'We're not caught yet,' said Temmi, unexpectedly fierce. 'But our only chance now is to escape the castle.'

'Quickly—inside and close the door,' cried Agna. 'We'll go by the secret passageway.'

Chapter Thirteen

Taking care not to look at the murderous icicle, Agna crossed to the ice bed and touched one of the corner posts. Immediately the whole bed slid back, revealing a flight of steps carved into the solid ice floor.

Temmi peered down it. 'Is the passageway really secret?' he asked.

'If you don't mind, I'd rather ask questions about it on the inside,' said Mudsniff worriedly. In the corridor they could hear angry voices approaching, with many wolves snarling bad-temperedly alongside.

'Come on,' said Agna. 'Hurry down, all of you.' She followed last, closing the opening not with a push but with a touch as before.

At once the light grew grey and dull, coming as it did through thick rippled ice. The roof was low enough to reach up and touch; and Temmi had to hold Cush who growled softly because to him the passageway was no better than a cage.

Without anyone seeing, they returned briefly to the nursery to snatch their warmest boots and cloaks (Agna had to borrow hers) and then it was back into the passage.

'This way,' said Agna. She let the others go by and hung back a little, ready to enjoy their amazement when they went round the next bend. And then they were there. Despite the urgency of the moment, Temmi stopped and gasped.

The passageway had only two walls and a floor, with the walls meeting overhead in a point. Because of its special shape the light was split into striking rainbow colours, one colour running into the next like thick wet paint. They shimmered, almost alive and certainly magical. Reaching out a hand Temmi found he could touch them; and just as surprising he could taste and smell the colours too. Green was mint, orange was spicy ginger (or sometimes nutmeg); yellow was as sweet as sugar. (For the dwarfs, however, the same colours were cabbage, tobacco, and tripe—and for Cush were different again, possibly a selection of his favourite fish!)

When Temmi next looked, the dwarfs were busy licking at the walls and had to be dragged away.

'Oh, let us stay—just a bit longer!' wailed Kobble who was especially fond of tripe.

'No,' said Temmi firmly. 'Not unless you want to end up as wolves' meat.'

With the help of Agna he managed to drive the dwarfs around the corner, where they found themselves starting down a long flight of narrow steps, the ice around them once more colourless and drab.

At the bottom of the steps the party came to an unexpected halt, the way ahead blocked by icicles that hung from roof to floor. The icicles were as gnarled as tree roots and far too thick to be broken with their hands—not that this stopped Wormlugs from trying, because biggest and oldest naturally meant strongest too.

'Ugh!' he exclaimed, finally admitting defeat.

Brushing him aside, Agna stepped up and began running her fingers down the icy pillars. At her touch each one made a different sound. Her hands worked faster and faster until the whole passageway was singing. Then the icicles lifted—all together, like a portcullis. Staring out through the gateway, Temmi saw dreary snowland, but to reach it they first had to cross the deep ravine that went around the castle like a moat, and the only way of doing that was by a worryingly narrow ice bridge.

'Don't look down,' called Agna crossing so nimbly that she made it look ridiculously easy.

The dwarfs bullied Kobble into going next, and only when he had reached the other side were they happy to follow. Temmi came last after releasing Cush; and as he crossed with his arms outstretched like a man on a tightrope, Cush hovered beside him giving him encouragement.

Once Temmi had jumped to safety they all stood together in the shadow of the castle, grinning and looking so pleased with themselves for having escaped it, that it took a dash of Mudsniff's gloom to bring them back to their senses again.

'This won't do us the slightest bit of good,' he announced. 'The minute we try to make for the forest we shall stand out against the snow like ants on sugar.'

Temmi saw what he meant, but as they couldn't fly he wondered how else it could be done? Then he noticed Agna take something from her pocket. It looked like a tiny clear icicle. She held the narrowest, most pointed end to her lips and her cheeks filled out as if she were blowing a horn— only it didn't make a sound.

Three times she did this, leaving Temmi wondering why and annoyed at losing so many precious minutes. Then he heard something approach, and turning around at last understood what Agna had done. She had called up the Queen's herd of reindeer; and now the animals stood before them, their antlers forming a prickly wall and their sweet hay-scented breath coming in steamy gasps.

'Quickly, get in amongst them,' cried Agna. 'They will get us to the forest unseen.'

The reindeer seemed to know what to do. They set off, walking slowly in a tight group towards the trees. They were not afraid of young bears, dwarfs, or children, yet neither did they trample or jostle them; and they were so large that no one had to stoop or bow their head. Reaching the forest eaves, the herd simply turned and walked away in a different direction, leaving Temmi and the others safe under cover of the trees.

Straight away they ran deeper into the forest until all sight of the castle was lost.

'What do we do now?' asked Flywick.

'We walk,' said Temmi, who as he went striding off knew it was only a matter of time before Tin Nose came after them—and the wolves too, of course. If only their tracks didn't show quite so clearly in the snow . . .

Temmi led the way through the forest, weaving in and out of the trees. The others followed him in a silent line, nobody feeling much like talking. It was all so dull and dreary, especially after the helter-skelter excitement of the earlier part of the day. And when the journey wasn't dull and dreary it was because of shadows and innocent sounds that gave them unpleasant jolts. Temmi knew he drove them hard, never letting them rest for more than ten minutes at a time, and then without food and with only ice melted in their mouths to drink. But he couldn't risk their staying so close to the castle.

By late afternoon the first shadows of night were forming. The silent trees stood like cones of snow, dark about their bases, glinting starlight at their crowns. Too tired to drag her feet another step, Agna simply stopped and her weary body sank to the ground.

'I can't go any further,' she gasped. 'I *can't*.' And she bowed her head in shame.

It was then, in the distance, they heard the full-throated cry of a wolf. Mudsniff nervously chewed his beard and Kobble's bottom lip trembled.

'Come on,' said Temmi harshly, and crossing over he roughly dragged Agna to her feet.

They set off again, now more frightened than tired: knowing that wolves run their best in darkness. They hadn't gone above a hundred steps more when the forest ended abruptly and before them stretched a frozen river, its far side thronged with snowy pines.

Temmi went to scramble down its bank, but Agna stopped him.

'*No!* We mustn't cross here,' she said. She sounded so certain that Temmi climbed back up again, obeying her without question.

Closely they followed the river, Agna stopping now and then to listen. Listen to what? wondered Temmi. *The ice?* He and the dwarfs were also listening. Listening to the howling wolves sounding nearer by the minute.

'We have to cross the river soon,' he blurted out angrily. 'The moon is up. They will spot us stepping out from the trees.'

'Not here,' replied Agna firmly, her head turned like a hunter ready to catch the smallest sound.

The dwarfs crowded together, trembling and frightened; pulling up their beards over their faces as if trying to hide. Then Agna stopped. She stood absolutely still, her small face white in the moonlight, her eyes closed. 'This is the place,' she told them a moment later.

The dwarfs swarmed forward.

'No!' shrieked Agna. 'It's important to cross one at a time.'

Temmi stared at her, unable to understand; and yet there was something about her that convinced him she was right.

'I'll go first,' said Wormlugs. 'It's proper for the biggest and oldest to lead the way.'

'Save your breath for running,' said Temmi. He could hear the wolves fast closing in around them, calling out for the joy of the hunt. No doubt this added speed to Wormlugs's legs, and a minute later Temmi watched him scramble up the far bank.

Crumbtoot went next, swiftly followed by Mudsniff, Flywick, and Kobble. Before Agna could argue, Temmi shoved her after them. 'Hurry,' he whispered.

Agna streaked out across the ice, running sure-footedly until she was safely upon the other side. Now it was Temmi's turn—

Yet as he was about to follow, he heard a sound so close it sent him slithering wildly down the bank, stones and snow spilling before him and his feet slipping on the ribbed ice.

In the shadows of the trees on the opposite side, Agna and the dwarfs watched with growing concern. They saw Temmi reach the river's halfway point—but so too did a far less friendly pair of eyes. A dark shape appeared and flung itself off the high bank behind him, hitting the ice and, still crouched, hurtling over the slippery surface until it was snapping at Temmi's heels.

'*Frostbite!*' growled Wormlugs; and he kicked away the snow until he found a good sized pebble. He felt its weight in his hand, took aim, then hurled it with all his might. It struck Frostbite on the shoulder. The wolf staggered and fell, howling with pain and surprise.

Hands meanwhile reached down to pull Temmi to safety.

'Look!' shouted Wormlugs pointing back over the way.

Onto the ice now poured shadowy men with spears.

Flywick shuddered. 'And there's Tin Nose himself.'

With sword drawn, Tin Nose led his men

forward, eager wolves at their feet. There were so many of them! But then something appeared to be wrong. In the middle of the river they came to an abrupt halt, looking around them fearfully. Too late some men and wolves turned to dash back to land—but an ugly crack in the ice ran faster and overtook them. With the crack came a harsh splitting sound and the slurp of water—then before they knew it the river's solid surface broke up into a jigsaw of tiny islands that drifted apart or bumped together.

On each island a scattering of Tin Nose's people suddenly found themselves clinging for their lives. But the ice was unsteady and had only to tip a little to set wolf claws scrabbling or throw men off balance—and then with a scream they'd slide over the edge to be quickly swallowed by the deep, black water.

Crouched and defeated, Tin Nose was hopelessly adrift. He saw Temmi watching him and tried to stand before thinking better of it.

'Don't believe you are safe yet, boy!' he roared. 'Best you keep checking over your shoulder! Best you sleep with one eye open looking out for me. For I shall come. Be sure of it—*I shall come*.'

His threat was more chilling than the night.

'Come on,' said Temmi to his friends. 'We waste good time here.' And as he turned he suddenly realized something.

Cush was missing. In fact Temmi was unable to remember the last time he had seen him.

Chapter Fourteen

Only after they had gone several more miles and were once again deep in the forest, did Temmi dare risk their stopping and setting up camp for the night. The damp twigs took a while to get going into a blaze, yet once they had, there was enough wood lying around to keep the fire burning until morning. Of course they still had nothing to eat, so the dwarfs smoked their pipes, warming their fingers around the pipes' clay bowls.

Wormlugs was in a bullish mood. 'Did you see how I hurled that great boulder?' he boasted. 'And did you see Frostbite jump? I must be one of the best shots in the whole world . . . Why, I wouldn't be surprised if I didn't have the sharpest eyes too. You can't have one without the other . . . '

The dwarfs nodded sleepily. Wormlugs pinched Kobble because he did not nod as well as he might—but Kobble was already asleep.

Temmi sat a little apart from the group, glancing up from time to time at the branches. Agna knew who he was looking for. She crossed over and sat on the log beside him, throwing her cloak around his shoulders so they both could share its warmth.

'Cush is probably quite safe, you know,' she said.

He glared up. '*Probably?*'

'Oh—I mean I'm certain that he is,' she added quickly. 'I expect he took fright when the wolves were closing in.'

Temmi nodded stiffly. He supposed she was right. Cush never did like the wolves, especially after what Frostbite did to him. Besides, thought Temmi, hadn't he always promised Cush his freedom and now he had it . . . But somehow he believed the moment would be rather wonderful—like the giving of a special gift. He smiled bitterly. Did he expect Cush to be thankful? He was only a bear after all and why should a bear understand such things?

'I hope Cush manages to find his way back to his father,' he said softly. 'It's a long way, even to fly.'

'Animals can be a lot cleverer than we think,' said Agna.

They were silent for a while, listening to the fire speak to them in crackles—as if it was telling them a story. Perhaps it was the one about the little flame who grew up to be a raging forest fire. Now and again the fire opened its mouth too wide and sparks flew out, fiercely bright among the stars.

Temmi gazed thoughtfully into the flames. 'Do you think we have seen the last of Tin Nose?' he asked.

Agna shrugged. 'At the moment I can't think of anything but food, *hot, cooked* food. I'm so hungry.'

Hearing her words, the dwarfs stirred restlessly.

'Food,' groaned Crumbtoot. 'What I wouldn't give for a few rashers of fried bacon—all sizzling and golden.'

'No,' said Flywick. 'A nice pork chop and the crackling just so.'

'Kidneys!' exclaimed Mudsniff. 'Slithering and chasing each other around the pan.'

Their squabble was suddenly interrupted by Kobble's loud snore. With a smirk Wormlugs dropped a twig into his mouth making him splutter.

'I think we'd all better get some sleep too,' said Temmi. 'We may feel better for it and tomorrow's journey is not going to be any easier.'

At the time Temmi had no way of knowing just how true his words would be. The journey certainly got no better, in fact it got a great deal worse. Leaving the shelter of the forest, they moved out on to the plains where snow was heaped up and the wind never grew tired of its own bullying voice; and whenever anyone lifted their head to see an end to it, the whiteness simply ran on and on to the horizon, hurting their eyes.

They were cold at every moment, of course, worn out by it, even Agna who had lived most of her life in the cold. But they always felt better with some hot food inside them.

In this, the rivers and lakes were as good as larders, providing all the fish they could eat, once Temmi had managed to smash a hole through the ice and lower his line. At first he struggled because he had no bait, but with the help of some hairs from Flywick's beard he made a lure and then they simply waited.

Five minutes later Temmi felt a tug and knew he had caught something.

Never was a fish landed with such excitement and applause as the one that was caught with those useful whiskers. After that it was much easier, as Temmi was able to use scraps of flesh to catch other fish.

'I think I shall turn into a fish myself if I have to eat another one,' grumbled Mudsniff several meals later.

'Why not?' said Crumbtoot. 'You already smell like one.'

But nobody really minded too much. They were so thankful to have food at all.

They trudged on, the second day sluggishly moving into the third day and dragging on into the fourth. Now and again Temmi caught himself glancing up in the hope of catching sight of Cush, a hard habit to break; while at night he dreamed of Cush. In his dreams he was flying beside the bear, high above the trees. But in truth, all that ever came from the sky were snow flurries.

On the fourth night they built camp on a narrow ledge of land, with a great sheltering mountain rising up on one side, and a canyon on the other, dropping down onto jagged rocks far below. In the sky over the mountains the northern lights shimmered like the hem of heaven.

Despite the cold, Temmi kept himself cheerful by thinking of his father and his village, and how he would feel when he saw them again.

The fire burned brightly, and the fish he had caught the previous day spat in the heat of the flames. The dwarfs dozed, crushed up together like sparrows, their heads resting on each other's shoulders; and Agna stooped to pick up more sticks for the fire.

Then she dropped them with a loud gasp.

The dwarfs wriggled awake at once, and Temmi spun around.

On the edge of the light, calmly watching, sat Frostbite and the wolf pack.

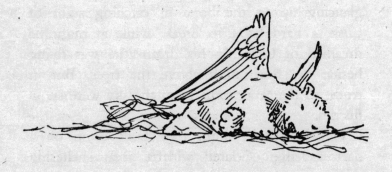

Chapter Fifteen

Having no weapons to protect themselves, the company did what Temmi did and snatched burning sticks from the fire, which against wild animals are as good as swords. However, Wormlugs was so busy running back and forth yelling 'Wolves! Wolves!' that Frostbite was able to take a daring chance. With a bound he came flying through the air, pinning the unfortunate dwarf to the ground; then roughly seizing him in his jaws, he began dragging him away from the light.

'Help! Help!' shouted the terrified Wormlugs.

It was horrible to hear him shout and squeal and not be able to do anything about it because the other wolves now pressed in, growling and pawing.

'I'm going to be eaten!' wailed Wormlugs.

'Hang on! Hang on, Wormlugs!' shouted Kobble, swishing his fiery stick left and right— until a couple of young wolves jerked back. Then he dashed through the space over to where Wormlugs lay clenched in Frostbite's jaws.

'*Take that*, you big bully!' yelled Kobble stabbing the wolf with his stick. But Frostbite refused to give up his hated enemy—even now with his great bushy tail set alight. Throwing away his stick, Kobble leapt at the wolf, and because he was so small and light, instantly became a rider upon the wolf's back.

This proved too much for Frostbite's dignity. Spitting out Wormlugs, he thrashed about in a frenzy—furious at the young dwarf and beside himself with terror at the fire which burned steadily and smokily and with the powerful smell of singed fur. No matter what he did, however, Kobble managed to stay in place, his voice jolted from him as he was bucked and twisted.

So grim was the struggle between dwarf and wolf, that the rest of the battle dwindled into a kind of half-hearted truce, while everyone (including the wolf pack) stood watching in disbelief.

Then Temmi saw Kobble faced a new danger and began to shout a warning. Agna joined in and all the dwarfs with her. They saw what blind rage stopped Frostbite from seeing. So busy was he trying to throw off the dwarf and escape the flames, that he had gone dangerously close to the edge of the steep drop onto the rocks below.

'Jump clear, Kobble!' they all called. 'Jump while you still can!'

But as they watched, the wolf's claws lost the last of their grip. Desperately Frostbite tried to scramble back to safety, only to find it was too late. The ice was glass smooth, and sliding out of control, he and the dwarf simply disappeared from sight into the dark, deep chasm . . .

The battle once more continued in earnest.

The wolves, far less bothered by the loss of their leader than the grief-stricken dwarfs were about Kobble, quickly took control. They rounded up the company like a flock of sheep and drove it away from the fire. Temmi, Agna, and the dwarfs drew closely together, their sticks making a wall of flames before them, but Temmi couldn't help worrying what would happen once the flames had burnt out. The wolves bared their teeth and came crowding forward, snapping and growling.

Inch by inch the company was driven back to the rocks that lay at the shadowy foot of the mountain. Temmi wondered why and glanced over his shoulder. The darkness there seemed as thick as fur. Then he saw something which jolted his whole body right down to the bones.

What he had caught at that moment was the winking glint of something small and gold deep among the rocky crevices. It was the moon's reflection off a false nose. *Tin Nose was lying in wait for them.*

'Ambush!' yelped Temmi. 'Tin Nose is at our backs!'

Seeing no reason to stay hidden any longer, Tin Nose stepped into view, his grinning men spreading out in a line with their spears.

Tin Nose pointed his sword at Temmi.

'This time, boy, there is no easy escape. I shall see to it that you're hacked into broken meat for the wolves.' Then he turned to Agna. 'As for you, girl, you shall know how traitors are dealt with and will wish for such a *comfortable* death too, as you lie in the ice—frozen alive for a thousand years.'

He lifted his sword; beneath it the dwarfs trembled.

'First K-Kobble and now us,' sobbed Mudsniff.

But before the blade could fall, something large and white and powerful swooped from the sky like an angel, striking Tin Nose with the tip of its wing and landing with a swirl of snow.

'Beog!' gasped Temmi, recognizing Cush's father. To the others it was the most fearsome creature they had ever seen.

The mighty bear stood before them, rearing up on his back legs, wings outstretched and dark eyes alert to every danger. At the sound of his roar the wolves bristled: they knew the bear could break them with just a glancing blow of his paw. The men had their spears, but none dared risk wounding the creature, since a wounded bear is like a whirlwind with claws.

Tin Nose lay sprawled in the snow where he had fallen, glaring up at Beog in hatred. Seeing his face, Crumbtoot gave a squeak of horror, for his golden nose had broken free, and without it his face was horribly like a skull.

'Is there not a man among you who will cut this creature down?' he shouted. He waited and when no one moved he leapt up gripping his sword.

Beog growled a soft warning and, as Tin Nose staggered towards him, his claws slashed down, sweeping the sword from Tin Nose's grasp as if a harmless twig in the hands of a child. Then he beat his wings hard, the down-draught nearly blowing the dwarfs off their feet; and, hovering about Tin Nose, he caught his cloak in his jaws, then rose up with the Witch's general struggling beneath him like a monkey on a rope. Rising higher and higher, Tin Nose cursed everyone there and swore bitter oaths of revenge.

'You think this is the last of me,' he raved. 'But Lord Thurbolt is made of metal and ice, he does not flinch like soft warm flesh.'

He pulled out a dagger and slashed at his cloak. Instantly it ripped all the way across and Tin Nose dropped free of Beog, kicking at the air as he fell, and disappearing into the chasm without a sound.

As if this were a sign to attack, white bears came swooping down from every side, scattering the wolves and driving the men in all directions. The flying bears chased after them, diving low, their swan-like wings outstretched and feathers ruffled; the air trembling behind them.

'We're saved!' cried Temmi throwing up his arms.

Feeling a playful nip on his neck, he spun around to meet Cush's face directly level with his own. The cub's whole body shook with pleasure and he immediately threw himself into Temmi's arms, licking his face all over and gently bumping him with his wings.

Temmi found himself laughing and crying with happiness; and seeing Agna watching him with a puzzled look on her face, realized this was another warmth she had never known before. *Love*. In its place she had been taught the coldness of duty.

The adult flying bears returned, some landing nearby, others circling above.

Wormlugs dabbed his eyes with his beard. 'Oh, if only Kobble were here to share this moment,' he sniffed. 'I would take his hand and shake it. Yes, I would warmly shake it and tell him that I, Wormlugs, may be the biggest and oldest dwarf, but he is certainly the bravest.'

Crumbtoot and Mudsniff nodded solemnly; Flywick took off his pointed hat and held it to his chest.

'Well, if you help me up, you can do these things for as long and as often as you like,' spoke a distant voice.

'It's Kobble's ghost!' hissed Mudsniff, covering his eyes. 'It's come to haunt us for the times we were unkind to him when he was alive.'

'Ghost be blowed!' replied the unghost-like voice. 'Although I may soon turn into one if you leave me stuck down here for much longer.'

They approached the cliff's icy edge taking extra special care. Lying on his stomach, Temmi spotted Kobble safe on a ledge just below him, and ordered the dwarfs to knot together three cloaks. This was done and lowered to Kobble. Then everyone lent a hand to fetch him back up to the top. When he appeared, the dwarfs pounced on him as if they were wolves, not with teeth and claws but with hugs and handshakes.

'I never knew you thought so much of me,' beamed Kobble, his face flushed and happy.

Now they were together again, Beog came lumbering forward, far less graceful on land than he was in the air. He pushed against Temmi nearly knocking him over, although he did not mean to be so rough; and every time Temmi turned away, Beog somehow managed to block him again by putting his side in front of him. At last Temmi understood why. Gently he pulled himself onto Beog's back, sitting behind the thick muscle where his wings joined.

Shyly other bears came up (Ocki and Abany, Snibpuss and Dorf . . .) one for each dwarf and one for Agna. They followed Temmi's example and minutes later were all sitting astride a flying bear.

Then Beog started to run: his paws pounded the ground and wings slowly fanned open. Temmi lay low along his back—and, happening to glance sideways, caught the tops of the trees sliding out of view.

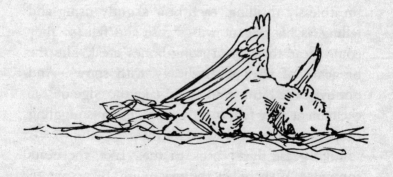

Chapter Sixteen

They rode with the wind blowing into their faces, gritty with snow. For Temmi and Agna and all of the dwarfs, travelling on the flying bears was breathlessly thrilling, each bear slightly rising and falling as his elegant wings rose and fell (so they could hear their great wing-bones creak like the branches of trees when heavy with snow). And not even the bitter cold could take the edge off the excitement they felt, it only sent Temmi snuggling deeper into Beog's downy warmth.

Like geese flying back to their lake, the bears formed a V-shape in the sky, with Beog out in front. Cush was the one blot on its neatness, keeping close beside Temmi—not the place

where a small cub should be. But good-naturedly
Beog let him stay; and Cush barked with joy, his
wings flapping madly to keep up, while his
father's wings never once changed their slow
steady beat.

Without stars to guide them and with all the
world below lost in darkness, Beog led the way by
smell, his wet nose sniffing and twitching at the
silvery-green coloured wind. He followed it for
many miles.

And then at last he spread his wings and kept
them spread. Behind him the other bears did the
same. Now they no longer flew but glided, the air
rushing hard over their feathers.

Temmi guessed this meant journey's end.
Impatiently he squinted up his eyes trying to see
better, trying to catch a glimpse of his village . . .
And then, in the distance, he saw glimmering
lights. Tears were blown from the corners of his
eyes, which might have been there because of the
cold, or might have been simple tears of happiness.

Suddenly, and without a signal, the bears broke
their straight lines, spiralling downwards. The
lake, forest, and huts of the village raced up to
meet them. Yet when Beog touched down, it was
done so softly that the fluffy snow came up in a
puff about his paws like wisps of smoke.

Sliding off his back, Temmi hugged the bear's neck. 'Thank you, Beog,' he whispered. 'Thank you for bringing me home.'

Not bothering to wait for the others, he ran stumblingly to the village. Cush looked as if he might fly after him, but Beog gave a low growl and Cush sadly turned back.

'Pa! Pa!' Temmi shouted as he reached the first hut.

Doors opened and heads peeped out. 'What's happening?' people asked.

'It's Temmi,' answered others amazed. 'He's come back to us. Temmi's returned from the dead.'

Temmi's father's hut was one of the last to open its door. When the door finally did open, Temmi was shocked by the face that peered out at him— it was so drawn and thin.

'Is that really you, Temmi?' his father croaked, dry lipped. 'It will be too cruel if this is just another dream and I wake up again by your empty bed.'

Temmi proved he was no dream by flying into his father's arms and with such force that he nearly knocked him down.

All around them Temmi could hear the villagers rushing up or calling out his name. Then he heard a suspicious voice shout, 'Strangers! Strangers in the village!'

Remembering the others, Temmi pulled free of his father's grasp. 'Agna and the dwarfs are my friends!' he protested. 'They mean no harm, Pa.'

'If they are your friends,' smiled his father stroking Temmi's hair, 'they are more than welcome.' And he called, 'Show our visitors to the longhouse. Temmi must have much to tell us.'

Their excitement growing, the villagers crowded into the long, low building. Agna and the dwarfs were already there; and as most villagers had never seen a dwarf before (let alone five!) many eyebrows were raised in surprise. However, the villagers were very polite, if a little unsure about them at first. The children were especially fascinated.

'Build up the fire,' ordered Temmi's father. 'Let's have light and warmth.'

Temmi glanced across at Agna and saw her nodding in agreement.

Then a silence fell as everyone waited to hear Temmi's story, which took a long time to tell; and when he introduced Agna as a queen and the adopted daughter of a witch, the villagers gasped 'Ooh' and stared at her as simple people would. Queens were even rarer than dwarfs.

A startled cry, however, brought silence again

just as quickly, and turning from Agna, everyone stared at old Cuddie and Ebleen his wife who held out her hand towards the girl, her fingers trembling.

'Agna . . . Don't you remember us?' asked the old woman in a voice hardly more than a whisper, but which carried to every corner of the longhouse. 'You were so young . . . a little child when you went missing in the forest.'

A buzz of excited whispers broke out around Agna, who stood perfectly still in the middle of it. She stared deep into the fire. It was the biggest and brightest fire she had ever seen—so naturally the warmest too. Its blue leaping flames were so long that they broke in two, but all in the flicker of a moment; and around its edge little demon tongues lapped hungrily. Faces and voices swirled inside Agna's head—and a frozen corner of her memory finally melted.

'I remember the forest,' she said slowly but as if to herself. 'The trees are green without any snow. Suddenly the Witch appears from behind a tree trunk and stands watching me. She asks if I want to ride on the back of one of her wolves. I don't, but am too afraid to say. The Witch picks me up—her hands are so cold that I shiver—and she puts me on to her biggest wolf. Then it begins to run. It runs so fast that I can't get off. I call out for my mother and father, but we have arrived at the snowy mountains and I begin to get so very cold—'

'Look at us!' pleaded Cuddie. 'Don't you remember now, child? We are your true father and mother. You were stolen from us over forty years ago.'

Again excited whispers broke out.

'But she is just a girl,' cried the blacksmith, bluntly saying what most other people thought. 'How can what you say be true if it happened such a long time ago?'

Agna gave the answer herself. 'In the Witch's lands,' she said, 'it is so cold that even passing time can freeze. I know this is so because Haggoth was over four hundred years old when she died.'

'And the Witch may have used her magic on Agna's memory to make her forget,' added Temmi.

Ebleen still stretched out her trembling hand. 'No matter how long, a mother will always know her own child,' she sobbed.

Agna felt all eyes upon her. She turned to Temmi. 'What shall I do?' she cried.

He smiled. 'Whatever the warmth inside you tells you.'

Agna didn't understand. She stepped up hesitantly to the old couple, meaning no more than to give them a respectful curtsy, but as she went by the fire she felt a curious glow inside that grew stronger by the second, quickening her breath and footsteps—and then she was running; and reaching her new-found mother and father, she caught them up in a great hug, sobbing uncontrollably until her face was red and blotchy.

Each dwarf sniffed and wiped away a tear. Wormlugs claimed a speck of ash had gone into his eye.

'Don't tell lies,' said Kobble gently pinching the older dwarf's cheek.

So much had happened that night—so much had been made better and put right that everyone was ready to celebrate, families bringing out their precious jars of ale and cider.

'To Temmi, Agna, and the dwarfs!' they cried. The dwarfs drank greedily, while the villagers stood by ready to top up their mugs with more. Strong drink had always been denied them at the Witch's castle since alcohol doesn't freeze and warms the drinker's insides.

'Whidge iv p-erfloctly twoo,' hiccuped Wormlugs, his nose glowing red.

Much, much later, in fact closer to morning

than midnight, the people returned to their huts. Amongst them were two reunited families.

Temmi and his father held each other as if one was unable to walk without the help of the other, which was rather awkward, not that they really noticed or cared.

Suddenly a deep roar stopped them in their tracks, and looking up at the sky Temmi saw Beog hovering over the roof tops, and Cush bobbing along beside him. The cub wagged his stumpy tail and barked.

'Cush has *his* father back too,' cried Temmi in delight. 'But I'll still come and visit you, Cush. Every day. And I'm sure Agna and the dwarfs will want to come with me.'

Seeming to understand, Cush swooped down, licked the boy's face in mid-flight and soared back up to his father. Then, together, they slowly wheeled around and made for home.

Extract from
Temmi and the Frost Dragon
ISBN 0 19 275252 9

Ollimun Nubb knew he was being studied from head to toe. He was used to it and considered it perfectly normal for ordinary folk to stare. And for that purpose he laid his wand across his knees so Temmi and Agna might have a better view of the designs upon it, seeing there a sun and moon at either end, similar to the tattoos upon his face—the moon in copper, the sun in ancient gold. The wizard sat very still waiting patiently until both curious youngsters were done.

'There,' he said, waving away the flies that had already begun to gather, buzzing in a cloud around the troll's ears. 'Now you know more about me than I do about you. Time you told me something about yourselves. Start with your names, that will be enough to begin with . . . *Boy*—you first.'

'Temmi, sir,' answered Temmi at once. 'Short for Temmithia.'

'And I'm Agna,' said she when he pointed his wand at her.

He nodded, satisfied. 'And the creature?'

'This is Cush,' said Temmi, hugging him. 'He's a flying bear.'

'So I see. It's quite a day for strange creatures. Luckily for flying bears and unluckily for trolls, I happen to know the good ones from the bad.'

Abruptly Agna said, 'It was you who put the protection around our village, wasn't it?'

'It was.'

'Why?'

For his answer Ollimun Nubb patted the troll. 'It will keep out the likes of him and his friends— at least for a while.'

Temmi frowned up at the troll's great muscles, considering the frightening strength that once it had.

'We nearly ended up as its dinner,' he said.

'Perhaps,' said the wizard coolly turning his gaze on Agna. 'It certainly meant to harm *you*, child. And possibly for the very same thing I can sense on you too.'

Temmi and Agna looked at each other, puzzled. The wizard went on.

'You have about you some object of great magical power.'

'No—' Agna started to say when she remembered a small trinket given to her by the

Witch-Queen of the High Witchlands when Agna was a princess there.

'Oh, you mean this,' she said taking out a small object of clearest ice. 'I call it Icicle—the ice never melts.'

'And it does do magic,' said Temmi. 'At the Witch's castle it helped us to escape, didn't it, Agna?'

She nodded. 'That was the last time I used it.'

Looking at him, it was hard for Temmi to judge what Ollimun Nubb was thinking just then, but certainly it was deep thoughts. He stretched out a hand, snake-skin bracelets on his wrist.

'May I?'

Agna glanced at Temmi who shrugged a *why not?*, then handed it over.

Carefully the wizard held up Icicle to the sun, examining every part of it. And then for closer inspection he put on a peculiar pair of spectacles which had a movable magnifying glass set into the frames: this he slid from his moon eye to his sun eye and back again, so one eye was always made to appear much larger than the other.

'Did the Witch tell you anything about it? he asked looking at Agna, his moon eye three times the size of his sun eye.

Agna shook her head. 'Only that it was precious

and would do magic for me, and one day I would find out just how great its powers are.'

'Did she ever warn you *not* to take it away from her lands?'

'No, but when she gave it to me she never expected I would leave her castle. Why do you ask? What is it that's so special about Icicle?

Temmi heard Ollimun Nubb splutter. '*Icicle.* Such a childish name. *It is not an icicle.* Nor is it something to be tucked away in your pocket like a toy. It is a dragon's lodestone, and it may surprise you to know that if you blow it like a trumpet it will summon a dragon.'

He saw the two youngsters look puzzled. He sighed.

'You have heard about dragons, haven't you?'

'Of course,' replied Temmi happily. 'They are big creatures and quite fierce too, so I hear.'

For a second time he heard Ollimun Nubb splutter. *Big-and-quite-fierce* . . . Ho, boy, they are *gigantic*! They are *fer-ocious*! They are the lord-king-emperor of every other living thing!' He sounded so excited that Cush lifted his head to stare at him. 'Neither good nor bad, they live for centuries and are almost impossible to kill. However, they have two weaknesses. The first is their love of treasure. Each dragon has its own treasure store, and every full moon must fly off to find more. The second weakness is much more complex . . . When a dragon hatches from its egg there is always one object more precious to it than a whole mountainful of ordinary treasure—*its lodestone*. I have known it to be a ring, or a lantern, or a sword. It may be something worth only a few pennies to you or me, but to a dragon it is priceless. You see, whoever owns that lodestone becomes the dragon's master.'

'And Icicle is one of these special objects?' whispered Agna, hugging her knees in excitement.

'Indeed. It belongs to a frost dragon called Grimskalk and was stolen from her many years ago by the old Witch-Queen. Grimskalk has been desperate to get it back ever since.'

'So I have a dragon—a dragon of my very own!'

Ollimun Nubb frowned. 'You would be foolish if you thought you could *own* a dragon—just as you would be unwise to try to use the lodestone to summon Grimskalk to appear. Only those with strong magical powers can ever hope to be master of a dragon. Those who have none are merely left with the dragon's curse.'

This, as well as the wizard's tone of voice, did not sound at all promising.

'What do you mean—*curse?*' asked Agna slowly.

'It is simple. To stop thieves, all dragons' treasure is cursed—the more precious the object the more terrible the curse. When you lived at the Witch's castle, the Witch had her own strong magic to disguise the lodestone and hide it from Grimskalk; more importantly, the Witch's magic prevented the curse from taking hold. Safe in her castle, the lodestone might not have been able to call the dragon, but it was still a marvellous magical object, which is why the Witch gave it to you. Ah, but once you took it away from the protection of her magic, matters changed . . . ' Ollimun Nubb closed his eyes for a moment and to Temmi's surprise he noticed that even his eyelids were tattooed! 'The dragon's curse is like a disease, child, and now it has spread from you to your village. The creatures of the Underworld are beginning to rise—are beginning to creep to the surface. The troll is proof of that. The dragon's curse is giving them the heart to come crawling up from their caves and holes in the deep dark depths below.'

'*Oh.*' Agna's expression dropped. 'In that case I shall get rid of Icicle—I'll get rid of it for good. Temmi will help me, won't you? We'll throw it into the deepest part of the lake—'

'It won't help you one little bit—the curse is too advanced. The only sure way to lift it now is for you—and only you—to return the lodestone to Grimskalk at the next full moon. That's when she is away from her mountain searching for new treasure. There is no other way.'

'None?' said Temmi.

'None,' said Ollimun Nubb firmly. 'Naturally I offer you my services as a guide . . . The question is, are you willing to travel along that long hard road with me?'

Agna didn't know quite what to say.

'What do *you* think?' she asked turning to Temmi.

He rubbed his chin. 'As I see it the choice is between trolls or dragons—or at least *a* dragon.'

This was no help at all to Agna, so for a long time she sat still, thinking hard: and by her expression Temmi knew she was arguing with herself over what she should do. Nobody rushed her.

At last she took back Icicle and put it safely into her pocket.

'Well?' demanded Temmi. 'If you're going to Grimskalk's mountain, I'm coming with you.'

'Good,' she said. 'I was hoping that you would.'